"Thanks for entertaining me."

"My rusty cooking skills appreciated the company."

"Your cooking's great, Jenny," Liam said, wishing he could say what was really on his mind. "Really... great."

In spite of himself, his words were laden with something that went beyond a mere compliment. All of his yearning was out there, ready for the next heartbeat, the next tight intake of breath. All he had to do was say what he was really feeling.

I want you, Jenny. I always have, and that's never going to change....

But saying it would only guarantee a replay of every relationship he'd attempted. He might make her happy for a month, but he could never be what he used to be—free and whole.

And he could never forget it.

Her eyes were wide, as if she expected him to go on.

As if she were terrified by the possibility of it...

D0012222

Dear Reader,

For this final book in THE SUDS CLUB miniseries, I'm very honored to have the chance to write about a heroine who finds the strength within herself, as well as through the encouragement of the man who loves her, to overcome great adversity. However, my fictional Jenny only reflects the bravery of many real-life people who discover themselves in the same situation as she. I'm proud to know a few of them, including my aunt Mary, who has survived breast cancer and serves as inspiration for me, my family and this book. There are many more heroes among us, too, and if you go to http://cms.komen.org/komen/index.htm, you'll find their stories, plus important information about fighting this disease.

Thank you so much for picking up this book, and also a huge thanks to all of you for reading this miniseries.

Here's to your own happy endings....

Crystal Green

www.crystal-green.com

FALLING FOR THE LONE WOLF

CRYSTAL GREEN

Silhouette®

SPECIAL EDITION®

Published by Silhouette Books

America's Publisher of Contemporary Romance

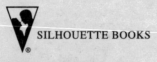

SILHOUETTE BOOKS
®

ISBN-13: 978-0-373-24932-9
ISBN-10:   0-373-24932-2

FALLING FOR THE LONE WOLF

Visit Silhouette Books at www.eHarlequin.com

Printed in U.S.A.

Books by Crystal Green

Silhouette Special Edition

Beloved Bachelor Dad #1374
*The Pregnant Bride #1440
*His Arch Enemy's Daughter #1455
*The Stranger She Married #1498
*There Goes the Bride #1522
**Her Montana Millionaire #1574
*The Black Sheep Heir #1587
The Millionaire's Secret Baby #1668
†A Tycoon in Texas #1670
††Past Imperfect #1724
The Last Cowboy #1752
The Playboy Takes a Wife #1838
Her Best Man #1850
§Mommy and the Millionaire #1887
§The Second-Chance Groom #1906
§Falling for the Lone Wolf #1932

Silhouette Romance

Her Gypsy Prince #1789

Silhouette Bombshell

The Huntress #28
Baited #112

Harlequin Blaze

Playmates #121
Born To Be Bad #179
Innuendo #261
Jinxed! #303
  "Tall, Dark & Temporary"
The Ultimate Bite #334
One for the Road #387

*Kane's Crossing
**Montana Mavericks: The Kingsleys
†The Fortunes of Texas: Reunion
††Most Likely To…
§The Suds Club

CRYSTAL GREEN

lives near Las Vegas, Nevada, where she writes for Silhouette Books' Special Edition line and Harlequin Books' Blaze series. She loves to read, overanalyze movies, do yoga and write about her travels and obsessions on her Web site. There, you can read about her trips on Route 66, as well as her visits to Japan and Italy. She loves to hear from her readers by e-mail through the Contact Crystal feature on her Web page, www.crystal-green.com.

To Aunt Mary, Ann Murray
and all you survivors out there.
Here's to your bravery and the admiration you inspire!

Chapter One

Liam McCree's day never really started until Jenny Hunter walked into the Laundromat.

Today, as always, she spiked his male radar, and his blood raced a little faster as he instinctively glanced up from his computer, at which he'd been tapping away in his corner of the Suds Club. His pulse beat in his ears, making him feel like he was being tossed around in one of the dryers.

From the first time Liam had seen her, over a year ago, when he'd initially moved into the neighborhood, his fantasy machine had been set to play reel after reel of Jenny 24/7—during the night, during the day… Nope, he never failed to fall asleep picturing how her short, smartly styled blond hair curled to a nape he'd love to nuzzle. How her blue eyes sparkled with the wit and dry humor that attracted so many friends…and probably admirers. How her plump red lips shaped into something sweet and cherrylike, as if ready to be tasted. How her pale skin covered a figure blessed with ample womanly curves.

Normally those curves were decorated with chic clothing when Jenny appeared in the Club. In fact, she liked to dress as fashionably as a 1950s movie goddess who lounged in a swank living room while she posed for photos in a feature article about domestic bliss.

But today, there was a difference in Jenny.

In his corner, Liam leaned his chair back against a dryer on the wall, quietly assessing her.

As she made her way to the seats in front of the television, her expression seemed dazed. Her arms were folded on her chest, and her usually perfect hair was pulled back into a tiny ponytail, as if she hadn't taken any care with it. She also wasn't wearing makeup—she didn't really need it, Liam thought—and the lack of her usual pizzazz made her seem…softer.

Sadder?

But most noticeably of all, she wore a drab, oversized, long-sleeved shirt over baggy khaki pants with sneakers.

Definitely not like Jenny at all.

Something was clearly up with her, but…

Well, Liam wasn't sure why he should involve himself by asking about her mood, since he seemed to be the bane of her existence. So he went back to typing in HTML codes for a Web site he was designing for a nearby jewelry boutique. Today, Web sites. Tomorrow, full-on small-business consulting. That was Liam's plan.

But Jenny kept drawing his attention, and maybe that made sense, since he'd often teased her about teaming up with him to start a consulting firm. After all, Jenny Hunter had a reputation as a crackerjack businesswoman, and she would be a great asset. She always brushed off his jokes, however, even if he wasn't entirely kidding.

She hadn't taken a seat yet. In fact, she seemed to be shying away from all the other Sudsers. A few ladies discreetly traded questioning glances when she wasn't looking, and this told Liam that they also suspected something was happening with the usually confident businesswoman.

Come to think of it, Liam reflected, Jenny had been getting quieter and more pensive lately, hadn't she?

The final minutes of a game show that preceded *Flamingo Beach*—the main reason everyone gathered in the Suds Club at this hour—played out on the TV. One of the women, an Eastern Indian named Evina, tried to draw Jenny into conversation. Yet the object of Liam's attention merely held up a finger, told Evina she would be right back, and headed straight for the drinks machine, as if retreating.

Her path would lead her past him, and his belly tightened.

He righted his plastic seat, the movement sending a twinge to his right leg, where underneath his worn jeans, scars covered an ache that was throbbing more than usual today.

Maybe the reminder of his injury—and the habit

of covering it with a smart-ass personality—urged him to stop Jenny as she passed. Or maybe it was because her sorrowful gaze somehow didn't sit right with him. Whatever it was, Liam closed the lid of his laptop, offering her a grin while folding his hands behind his head. "Halloween come a few weeks early this year?"

She slowed down, just now seeming to notice that he was in his usual corner. Then, as she came to a full stop, her eyes lost their haziness and seemed to focus.

In their blue depths, Liam detected the color of anxiety…maybe even fear. He'd seen the same hue in the mirror years ago, after his accident.

Should he ask her what was wrong?

"Your clothes," he continued, nodding toward her blasé garb. "It's…just a different look for a fashionista like you."

Okay, that was close to inquiring about her personal life. For him, anyway.

She frowned, glancing down at her outfit, then almost absently pulled her shirt away from her chest, as if trying to make her clothing even baggier. She was obviously not comfortable in them. Was not comfortable even being here today.

Liam knitted his brow, but he didn't venture another comment.

Could her attitude have something to do with how she'd missed her usual Wednesday-work-from-home lunch hour this week? She never failed to show up at the appointed time, but she'd been conspicuously absent yesterday.

He'd been all too cognizant of that.

"You had a lot of work going on yesterday?" he

asked. Translation: *What's with your change in schedule and appearance?*

Jenny swallowed, hesitated. Then a change seemed to take her over, as if she were forcing herself to put on some act. She even tilted her chin a little higher, taking the argumentative stance she always assumed around him.

But there was something missing—heart. Spirit.

"Yeah," she said. "I was really swamped with a project, and I needed every hour available to me. Today's better."

"Must've been some project."

"It was." Her eyes got that faraway look again. "Huge."

Liam motioned to his corner of the Laundromat. "Just set up your office in here. There's plenty of room, and you'll never miss *Flamingo Beach* at the Suds Club again."

He'd hoped to see a sign of the old Jenny: maybe she'd plant her hands on her hips, as she often did while bantering with him.

McCree, she would say, *squatting in a Laundromat instead of renting real office space might be the gypsy thing to do, but I need more organization. More room. More professionalism.*

But now she only ran a glance over him, as if she were seeing him for the first time: a guy in a corner, with a slight goatee, shaggy brown hair, comfortable clothes and that gypsy attitude.

His temperature rose and she looked away, catching herself.

Hell, Liam almost thought she was interested.

Doubtful.

"Things going okay at work?" he asked.

She was a hot dog at the Kendrick Corporation in San Francisco proper, where she dreamed up marketing plans for big accounts.

"McCree," she said, "if you're going to tease me about working for your hardly existent business today…"

"It'll exist."

"Oh, I don't doubt it." She gripped the hem of her shirt. "Just not with me."

"Hey." He leaned forward. The change in position sent a thread of discomfort through his leg, but he ignored it. "Anytime you want to get away from all the corporate red tape at Kendrick, you just let me know."

The offer was genuine, and she seemed to realize that for the first time. Her hands dropped to her sides as she turned her face away; then she nodded, biting her bottom lip.

Her innocent gesture blasted him. He'd imagined the feel of those swollen lips so many times, wished to experience the cherry taste of them. A million shivers danced over his skin as he told himself it would never happen, not with a woman who had always seemed to think he was more of an irritant than a true possibility.

Besides, Liam doubted he had it in him to make any woman happy in the long run, after she saw beneath all his coverings and witnessed the injuries, the damage.

But when Jenny's gaze met his, a jolt of electricity seemed to zap between them.

Then she looked away again.

A few heartbeats thudded by, marking the seconds, the burning aftermath.

Had she felt it, too?

He shifted in his seat again, and his leg screamed—a sharp reminder of his imperfections.

Of reality.

Meanwhile, Jenny's hands still hung at her sides, and her eyes had gone back to that empty look that blocked any sparks he'd seen during these past few seconds.

Strangely moved by the change, Liam found himself overstepping his bounds. "Jenny, is everything really okay with you?"

As her eyes widened—what, did she think she could hide it from him?—she twisted the hem of her shirt and pulled it away from her body, camouflaging every natural, beautiful curve.

"I'm fine," she said, her voice sounding choked.

Before he could follow up, she rushed toward the soda machine, digging into her pants pockets for money.

It felt as if the oxygen had been shoved out of his lungs. He was used to Jenny's shrugging him off and then eventually wandering past him again to continue whatever argument they'd been having before. But this time? He doubted she'd be back. Not when they both knew she was lying about being okay.

While Jenny kept her back to Liam, one of the Suds Club's regulars turned up the TV. *Flamingo Beach* was on, and everyone in the Laundromat had deserted their washers, their folding, and gravitated toward the seats in front of the screen. Earlier, they'd been guessing what might happen at Trina and Dash's wedding, but now there was respectful silence as the bride got ready to walk down the aisle.

Liam flipped up the top of his computer and reimmersed himself in his work.

By the time the bell on the Laundromat's door dinged, signaling the arrival of Mei Webb, Liam was already well into pretending to have no interest in the soap opera—or the people in the Suds Club—whatsoever.

Even though he was much too aware of Jenny, still standing with her back to him at the soda machine.

Jenny stared at the buttons on the vending machine. Water. Orange soda. Apple juice.

As she tried to concentrate on each offering, she rubbed her arms, hoping to calm the tremor that was running over her skin.

It was cold—that was all. The air outside was getting autumny, the leaves were turning, and she should've brought a jacket.

These shivers had absolutely nothing to do with Liam McCree. First of all, he wasn't her type. At all. Light-brown-eyed scoundrels who slacked around in grungy clothes didn't cut it for her. Just look at him—

Jenny didn't, but she could recall every detail of what he was wearing anyway. She was a clotheshorse—well, she usually was—so she noticed those types of things, and a long-sleeved shirt carelessly covered by a T-shirt worn with weathered jeans and beaten work boots made McCree a definite candidate for any and all worst-dressed lists. Honestly, she liked the clean-cut, suit-and-tie type, the patently ambitious man who walked the San Francisco financial district as if he owned it. McCree was the anti-Jenny man.

Then again, who was she to critique anyone's wardrobe with the way she looked?

Unattractive, dumpy…

In spite of herself, she chanced a slow glance at McCree, only to find him working away at his computer. Quickly she faced the vending machine again.

Had she expected him to be watching her or something? Based on what had happened a few minutes ago…

She concentrated on counting the quarters in her hand, telling herself that there hadn't been some explosive moment between them.

Please. McCree was just being his obnoxious self, baiting her, messing with her. Nothing more. There hadn't been a flash of awareness between them at all.

Because she couldn't be attractive to anyone now.

Taking a deep breath, Jenny heard her favorite soap in the background, but it sounded like a foreign language. Almost everything did.

And that was because of the mammogram results she'd gotten the day before yesterday.

Her throat lumped up, as if warping, just like her left breast had obviously done.

"There's an abnormal change," the radiologist had told her before advising a biopsy.

Then her doctor's voice took over in her mind. "But there's no reason to worry until we know for certain. Just relax in the meantime, Jennifer. That's the best thing you can do."

Sure. Relax.

She listlessly dropped the quarters into the machine, not knowing which drink button she would push. Fear ate away at her, muddling her head and making every decision seem as difficult as solving a quantum physics equation.

Then, thank God, she heard a familiar voice next to her.

"Hi, there," Mei said, touching Jenny's arm. "It's great to see you out and about."

Without further greeting, Jenny fell into her friend's waiting hug, burying her face in Mei's long, shiny, straight black hair and telling herself *not* to cry. She'd done enough of that Tuesday, after she'd gotten the news. Mei had been the only one besides Jenny's parents who knew that her doctor had found a lump in her breast, and she had come to the city to drive Jenny the other day and offer support at her appointment.

Although Jenny hadn't actually cried until they'd gotten back to her apartment, she had stifled some sobs and made an utter fool of herself at the appointment anyway. Jennifer Hunter—thirty-year-old cosmopolitan woman, successful businessperson…the one everybody thought was so self-sufficient and capable.

She was a major mess.

Luckily her schedule allowed her to work from home the day after the appointment, and she'd given herself permission to sit on the couch watching TV until she'd been up to attempting some work. And even though she'd taken a huge chance with her hard-case boss and called in sick today, she'd forced herself to stick to her routine and come to the Suds Club, even though she still felt like a zombie under the weight of all the terrifying worst-case scenarios her imagination was conjuring.

What if she needed radiation treatment? Or chemo? Or a mastectomy?

What if…?

She exhaled, pulling away from Mei, holding back more tears. She wasn't going to weep again, even if it felt like the right thing to do.

But the sympathetic look in Mei's dark eyes almost pushed Jenny over the edge.

Suddenly she felt even more uncomfortable in the oversized clothes she'd hidden herself in. She tugged at her shirt, pulling it away from her chest, only now realizing that she was attempting to negate what she might lose: her femininity.

And that didn't even begin to cover what else she might lose.

Mei gently grabbed Jenny's wrist, stopping her from pulling at her shirt anymore.

Jenny let go of the material. "Doesn't it cover up the lump?" she asked, her voice shaking slightly. She'd meant to seem light for Mei's sake, but it hadn't come out as a joke at all.

Her friend started to speak, but Jenny beat her to it.

"I just don't want anyone looking at my chest now, you know?"

"Oh, Jenny."

Mei had lowered her voice while keeping a hand on her friend's wrist. She sent a secretive glance over to one of the Laundromat's corners—Liam McCree's corner.

Jenny turned to glance at him, but he was so invested in his computer that she doubted he'd heard anything.

Or had he?

Her heart thwacked in her chest. McCree wasn't reacting to what she'd just said, but then again, it always seemed as if he saw right through her. Maybe he was used to her accidental revelations. Maybe he'd even sensed something about her earlier. Was that why he'd been asking all those questions and acting nice?

Great—that was the last thing she needed. It was hard enough to hide her devastation without McCree sidling into her business, too.

He just kept tapping away at his keyboard, though, and Jenny decided he truly hadn't heard a thing. Thank God.

She turned back to Mei, who said, "So you took off work today? Good. You deserve even more hooky time tomorrow."

Jenny shook her head and took care to lower her own voice. "I've got the Thayer account, and even though I've tried to work from home these past couple of days, I can't put it off any longer. Besides, my boss enforces a zero-tolerance absence policy, and I already used up most of my vacation and personal days when I helped my parents relocate back east a few months ago. When I took off Tuesday, it was my last official day *to* take off."

Mei kept her voice low. "But you can't be fired for taking days off in this situation."

Jenny bristled. "No, they wouldn't fire me for getting sick. It's just that—"

Anxiety chopped off her next words, but she reclaimed them.

"Mei, the last thing I want to do is announce what I'm going through to my boss, especially when this could just be a scare. I'm not going to be the 'sick girl' there."

Not when she'd worked so hard to be the "hotshot."

Not when that title gave her such a measure of comfort when she wasn't sure what else she had to hold on to.

Mei seemed to understand how important it was to keep her personal life under wraps for now. "Then what about taking today off?" she asked. "If your boss doesn't know what you're going through, won't he write you up?"

"Yes, but it'll be just one strike against me. Three, and I'd be out, but my anniversary's coming up in a couple of months, so I'll get more days off then." Jenny fidgeted with her shirt. "My latest account has been my life the last few months, and I'm way ahead of the game on it. There's no way I'm going to sabotage myself by needlessly bringing this into the office."

Mei touched Jenny's arm. "Why can't you just rest?"

She fisted her hands. "Because this account is important."

"But it shouldn't cost you your health," she said. "You need to take care of yourself."

"I need—"

Now Jenny cut *herself* off because she knew she could never explain just how much work had come to mean since she'd found the lump. She used to fill all her time with serial dating, but the lump had put an end to that: she'd even started pushing men away, because what if this turned into something more? What man would want to deal with her troubles and her losses?

What if, what if?

But work? Ah, work didn't present any such quandaries. By dedicating herself to succeeding at the Kendrick Corporation, she didn't have to compete with all the other women who would be whole and beautiful for the rest of their lives. Jenny ran with the guys on a different track, one dominated by brains, not boobs.

Besides, if she nailed the Thayer account, maybe she could forget about the upcoming biopsy…and anything that might happen afterward. Or maybe she would be such a success that attractiveness and sexuality wouldn't matter…?

And maybe her triumphs would define her when she wasn't quite sure how to define *herself* any longer.

Mei was patting her arm, and Jenny put her hand over her friend's.

"You don't have to tell me," Jenny said. "I'll think positively."

"And I'll help in any way I can."

"I know you will. Thank you." She smiled at Mei, so appreciative, but she desperately wanted to change the subject.

She pushed a button on the vending machine and a bottle came tumbling out. Apple juice. As Jenny grabbed it, Mei seemed to understand that it was time to let her be.

The Suds crowd was calling for them to sit down, but Jenny wasn't in a social mood, so she faked a cough and motioned that she was going to stay away for a moment.

"I'm saving a seat for you," Mei said as she took her place among their pals.

Jenny smiled at her friend, and the show started, encouraging everyone, including Mei, to turn around and watch. Since Jenny hadn't told any of the Sudsers but Mei about the lump, her secret-keeping had isolated her a little more every day, which felt strange since she was so used to being social.

She noticed that McCree had started to watch her again, and he had an odd look on his face—not the saucy, rakish look she was used to, either. It was more the expression of a man trying to understand something. Understand her.

In that moment Jenny realized that, lately, she had completely lost any idea of who she was or where she was going. That she was floating and she wasn't sure what she should grab to pull herself out of this daze.

When the Suds crowd applauded at the sight of Trina in her gorgeous wedding dress, Jenny gravitated toward them, glancing at McCree one last time, only to find that he was packing up his computer. Then he limped to the door, not saying goodbye to anyone.

Through the window Jenny watched him pass, not realizing that her pulse was thudding until it blocked out every other sound.

Liam headed toward his nearby apartment, which was housed in a redbrick complex covered with ivy. He could see it even from here, at the curb to the left of the Laundromat.

He stepped off of the sidewalk to cross the peaceful street, his bad leg paining him even more now, probably because rain was on its way; he could even smell the threat riding the air. At the same time, fog blocked the sun and offered a chill to go along with the orange-and-black Halloween decorations that ribboned the store windows.

A similar fog seemed to envelope him.

Although he'd pretended not to hear, he'd caught most of what Jenny and Mei had been talking about. But he still couldn't wrap his mind around it.

Doesn't it cover up the lump? I just don't want anyone looking at my chest now.

Now he knew why Jenny seemed to be a shell of her old self.

Liam only wished he could tell her that there were people who'd always think she was amazing, no matter what happened to her body.

And that he was one of them.

Chapter Two

The next day Jenny didn't roll out of bed until late morning, and even though she knew she'd traded this peace of mind for a second write-up at work, it felt damned good.

She'd followed Mei's advice, taking just *one* more day here at home, where she would still put in time on her project before going back to the office on Monday. She was sure that after the weekend she'd be psyched up enough to go full speed ahead on the Thayer account with the rest of her team.

The relaxation really would do her good.

She took a shower, then munched on leftovers from last night's Chinese takeout dinner and fixed a pot of healthy green tea from a box that had been lingering in the back of her cupboard for months. Although she'd purchased the tea during a trip to Chinatown with her visiting parents—who'd wanted to rush over here again at the news of the health crisis until Jenny had persuaded them to wait for a more detailed report—she had never found much use for nutritious food. So in spite of the tea's novelty, to the rear it had gone.

Now she regretted not taking better care of herself.

Who could say exactly what caused disease?

Sitting on the couch, she sipped her tea and stared at the walls of her two-bedroom apartment. She absently scanned its deep green walls, white and beige furnishings, angular sculptures, and mirrors here and there. Classic modern with no visual clutter—it was her to a tee.

Or…it had been.

She touched the hem of yet another oversized buttondown she'd chosen to wear today for its covering mercy. Like yesterday's shirt, it'd belonged to Franklin, the man she'd dated for three years before they'd broken up. That had been two years ago, and there'd been no hard feelings. In fact, saying goodbye had been much too easy, because she'd truly believed that there might be someone else out there who made her more passionate, made her blood simmer whenever she was near him.

Yet that was before, and this was now.

She kept staring, then realized that the silence was giving all her fears too much opportunity to scream through her head. She turned on the TV.

Good enough for now. Maybe she could stay like this for hours: blanking out with the help of some skin-care infomercial while she sat feeling sorry for herself. But she soon got much too bored, and she decided she needed some actual stimulation.

After Jenny freshened up and pulled back her dried hair, she left the apartment for the Laundromat.

She was going to push herself to get out of this funk. Her old self would've been terribly disappointed if she didn't make the effort, and she was missing the old Jenny who'd always had such fun at the Suds Club.

Maybe she'd find her there.

She walked the short distance to the Laundromat, the sky gray and swelling with coming rain.

Picking up her pace, she huddled into the waterproof jacket she'd grabbed on the way out. But when she closed in on the Club's door, she came to a halt. So did something in her chest—something that dropped to her stomach and swirled in lazy circles.

McCree was just stepping onto the sidewalk. Or maybe a better description would be limping. Since he normally arrived before and departed after everyone else—except for yesterday—no one ever actually saw him walking around. He worked in the same corner for hours, and he hid his injury so well she tended to forget it even existed. The fact that no one really ever talked about his leg—probably because he'd never offered details about it—only made it easier to ignore.

He saw her standing there gaping at his limp, and his skin went ruddy, his jaw clenching as he positioned his shoulder-strapped computer case like a shield that might ricochet her focus away from his leg.

Embarrassed at her lack of couth, she smiled, wedging her hands into her deep jacket pockets.

"Don't you usually get here earlier to start your computer marathon?" she asked, nodding at the Club's glass door.

"I'm running late today. Had to take a phone call about a business loan, and I didn't want to do it here."

She expected that, at any moment, he would bust out in a grin, once again becoming the McCree who tested her nerves just by existing.

But instead, he seemed to be searching her face for... For what?

Their eyes locked, and the same sharp awareness she'd felt yesterday when they'd made prolonged eye contact buzzed between them.

She tore her gaze away. This was *McCree,* the water to her oil. Buzzing wasn't supposed to happen when he was around. It wasn't supposed to happen with her in these clothes and no makeup.

Jenny cleared her throat, noticing that McCree hadn't made any move toward the door. Was it because he didn't want her to see him walking anymore?

All right—she would just scuttle inside and let him be. But before she could do that, he spoke.

"No potluck for you today?" he asked.

She tilted her head, not so much at the question, but at his tone. Usually, his voice was honed by that teasing edge. Now, it was...gentler.

Had he heard her talking to Mei yesterday? McCree's pity wouldn't sit well with her.

"Potluck," she repeated, raising her chin a notch. It was her regular, instinctive, talk-to-McCree stance.

He grinned a little, as if recognizing her rules of engagement. Still, the smart-ass didn't emerge, and that continued to throw her off balance.

"On Fridays," he said. "You know everyone brings chow—Crock-Pot beef, pasta, pies. I think there's an autumn theme today."

Duh, Jenny. Although she was rarely here on Fridays, she knew darned well about the potlucks. If her head had been together, she would've remembered.

"Maybe I should run to the market." There was one a couple doors down. "An autumn theme, you say?"

"Don't sweat it."

Then she noticed that he didn't have anything resembling food, either, unless it was in his computer case.

"What did you bring?" she asked.

He raised an eyebrow at her, and it made him look more McCree-ish than usual.

Devilish.

Her stomach went goofy and she pulled her jacket tighter around her.

"Naturally," she said, "you wouldn't deign to eat at the potluck, would you?"

"Naturally."

"In fact," she said, seeing an opening to discover whether he'd overheard her news yesterday, "you're pretty comfortable in that corner of yours, pretending you couldn't care less about the soap opera and whatever else is going on in the room."

"I *don't* care." He looked away from her.

But then, slowly, his gaze dragged back until it connected to hers again, just like yesterday. It was as if they couldn't help it.

Zzzzzzzinnnnng—

Jenny caught her breath at what she saw in his light brown eyes. Emotion—indescribable, but shattering all the same.

Had he always looked at her like this?

He couldn't have. She would've noticed. Or maybe she'd already convinced herself that he wasn't her type, and she treated him accordingly.

At any rate, she didn't have the energy for this now, not with the Thayer account, not with the upheaval in her personal life.

This time, both of them cleared their throats. And when they moved toward the door at the same instant, they almost ran into each other.

They hesitated.

He motioned for her to go first, but she wanted to ask one more question.

"McCree?" His last name provided a buffer. It kept things…casual.

He obviously understood her tactics, and he almost seemed relieved that she was using them. "Yes, Hunter?"

There. Good. Familiar, comfortable ground.

"Yesterday, when Mei and I were talking—"

Without warning, the Laundromat door opened, the bell dinging. A twenty-something mother named Charlotte bustled out, coming between them.

"I forgot my chocolate sauce," she said as she headed toward the market. "What's my Bundt cake without it?"

By the time Jenny refocused on McCree, all opportunity for noting his initial reaction to her half question had disappeared. He was frowning, and she couldn't tell if his expression was an attempt to make her think he didn't know what she was leading up to or if it was genuine.

"Go on," he said.

Jenny fidgeted with her jacket, realizing that she was pulling it away from her chest. "Did you happen to overhear what Mei and I were talking about by the vending machine?"

His careless, baffled shrug was the only answer.

She didn't elaborate, of course, and he looked miffed at that. But if he really hadn't heard, she needed to leave it alone.

With a casual "Okay, then," she opened the door and went inside, not waiting around for him to lob any un-settling questions, then headed for Mei, who was folding a load of whites.

So it appeared McCree didn't know, and thank God for that, because the longer Jenny could contain her secret, the better off she would be.

And she kept telling herself that, too, until it sounded like the truth.

As more Sudsers arrived, Liam saw how the growing selection of potluck items seemed to get to Jenny.

It wasn't long before she went to the market and returned with a pecan pie. While she sliced it with a borrowed knife, Jenny remarked that she didn't cook much anyway, and she was saving them from being polite about stomaching her food.

The flash of humor made Liam grin to himself, but when she sought an isolated chair and hunkered into it while wrapped up in her massive yellow jacket, he recalled what he'd heard her tell Mei yesterday.

A lump…

Earlier, when they'd been outside together, he could've sworn that, once again, he had helped her to forget about her worries for a short time. She had seemed like the old, prideful Jenny-warrior, and the sight of that had affected him.

Actually, Liam had even felt useful, but he'd also known the feeling wouldn't last—it never did when it came to women. Proof of that was sitting across the room from him now, as Jenny continued to remove herself from everyone else by creating her own corner.

One that resembled Liam's way too much.

He wished he could tell her she could depend on him to keep her secret, that he would even help out if she wanted.

But no. Wouldn't happen.

For the next hour, *Flamingo Beach* whipped the crowd into excited talkiness. Delia, the villainess, was wreaking havoc on Dash and Trina's wedding. At the same time, the Sudsers demolished the potluck offerings and made subtle attempts to draw Jenny further into the group. But she remained just outside of them, not eating anything, merely keeping her eyes on the TV. And when she left early, hugging Mei in farewell and waving to the rest of the crowd, Liam slipped out, too.

Since Jenny was strolling—slowly, much too slowly—he managed to catch up to her, computer, limp and all. He did his best to hide the drag of his leg as he spoke. "Was the show too exciting to tolerate?"

At first, she seemed surprised at his presence: her blue eyes even lit up. Then she looked at him in silent inquiry. *Why're* you *here, Mortal Enemy?*

There was the old spirit.

He shrugged while they waited for the traffic light to turn green. "Now that things are starting to take shape with my business, I've got phone calls to make at home."

"Likely excuse," she said, her tone almost light. Almost. "I'll bet you're cutting work early, McCree. Won't the boss be angry with you?"

"The boss knows he might as well be kind to the employees every once in a while. He's a real tough nut, but he can be all right on occasion."

"He only has one employee to please."

She cocked her head toward Liam, looking at both boss and employee of his modest company. But that would change, Liam thought. Just as soon as he could launch McCree and Associates, Solutions for Businesses.

The light changed and they crossed the street. She kept her pace deliberate so he could keep up. He didn't know whether to be thankful or insulted.

Bitterness speared him, momentary but familiar. If only he could move like he used to, before the accident. She would see a different man—one who ran, one who had felt free only when the adrenaline was pumping through him.

When the welcome smell of roasted chicken and barbecued ribs came to him, he allowed it to displace the hard feelings. No use dwelling on things that would never change.

The aromas only got stronger as they reached Lavender Lane, where some small white tents announced the weekly farmers' market that was held on the closed-off street.

Jenny veered toward it. "I'm usually in the city at this time of day, so I forget… They'll have organic stuff here, huh?"

"Right. Produce, vitamins, herbs…organic heaven."

She stopped at the entrance and assessed the people streaming through the aisles, the tents offering everything from homemade soaps and crafts to fresh-baked breads to exotic foods. To the right, a fruit stand boasted piles of temptations like grapes, apples and pears.

"I've been thinking of eating better," she said. "You know how it is in offices—grab a coffee and muffin from the snack cart in the morning, then an iceberg salad with all the fixings—totally deceptive healthwise—at noon. Then takeout at night because I'm still in the office so late."

Was she thinking of improving her diet to counteract any possible cancer?

"You should enter the fray," he said, fighting the sudden rawness in his throat. "Support your local farmers, eat well. All that."

"Sounds good to me."

Jenny turned to scan him, and he was all too aware of his scruffy outfit, his gypsy hair and attitude. He was a far cry from her high-class bearing—even if she was wearing that dreary jacket and clothing.

A secretive smile tilted her lips, making him wonder what was running through her mind as she walked toward the fruit stand, where there were samples among the piles of vivid produce.

"Pluots," she said, picking a portion—which resembled a plum more than the apricot it had been crossed with—from a paper tray. "You know, I've always wanted to try one of these, but I've never gotten around to it. These might be the last of the harvest."

When she slid it into her mouth, she closed her eyes and smiled. "Mmm."

Liam's body went "mmm," too. It tensed, it tightened, it devoured the way she licked her lips afterward. His nighttime fantasies grew bold with colored life as he imagined leaning over to taste the last of the fruit from her mouth—

But the rustle of a plastic bag as Jenny grabbed it brought him back to reality.

She stuffed several fruits into it. "This is fun."

"You gonna eat all those before they spoil?"

As if to spite him, she deposited one more pluot into her bag before tying it. Then she flashed him a grin and sampled a grape, thoroughly enjoying that, too.

Knowing they might be here for a while, Liam filled a bag of his own, then paid for it while Jenny got behind him in line and reached for her wallet.

"Don't worry," he told her. "I've got it."

She looked stunned at his offer to pay. Did it seem as if he was being too nice?

As if he'd truly overheard her secret and was compensating for it?

Hell, she already suspected he knew about her lump. He'd lied—actually *lied*—to preserve this new thing they had going. A "thing" that defied explanation.

"It's okay, McCree," she said, continuing to get out her wallet.

As she paid for her own items, he tried not to let her refusal sting, even slightly.

But it did, even though he shoved it aside.

When they left the fruit stand, he saw how Jenny's interest was piqued by each tent they passed, at how her walk seemed a little looser, as if she had found some sunshine in the sky and in herself, as well.

But a rumble of thunder reminded him otherwise. So did the aching of his leg.

They came to a stand that sold Afghan food, and as Jenny perused the offerings—sampling them, of course—he took the opportunity to rest and put his weight on his good leg. She bought a bag of moong dal grains, then some paratha—a bread that looked like giant tortillas, stuffed with pumpkin, in this case—as well as tomato chutney sauce. Afterward, she turned to Liam, opening her bag as if to share.

But she stopped short when she noticed his pose.

Damn it, couldn't he hide his discomfort better than this?

Without a word, she headed for an empty bench, then plopped down to go through her booty. And even though it seemed as if that were her sole purpose, he knew better.

Nevertheless, he sat.

She took out the package of moong dal. "Did you sample this? It's really good. They almost taste like tiny potato chips when you have them right out of the bag."

He grunted in response, distracted by his leg.

Jenny set the bag on her lap. "You're hurting, aren't you."

Not a question, but a statement—one he couldn't deny.

"It happens sometimes," he said, looking at the sky. Rain was coming soon. Very soon. "You know how they say old men can feel bad weather in their bones?"

"As if you're so old." Jenny packed the moong dal away, still not looking at him. "McCree…"

She stopped, as if checking herself.

"What?" he asked, knowing what was coming and dreading it.

Biting her lower lip again, she seemed to debate with herself before finally asking, "What happened with your leg?"

He'd expected the punch of such a question to be cruel, yet it eased between them like something inevitable, like the rain that would be on them soon after the next shake of thunder. He caught her glancing at the way he was holding his leg, nursing it, and he saw the barely banked sorrow. Was she picturing what might happen to her own body, how it might end up being damaged, too?

He didn't talk about his leg to many people—just his parents, really. And a few friends he shot hoops with on good days. It was too private. Too…painful.

But now, as she waited for him to answer with that confusion—a longing for answers—in her gaze, Liam knew he would do anything for Jenny.

Even if it meant revealing the last part of himself that he ever wanted her to see.

Chapter Three

Jenny couldn't believe she'd asked McCree such a personal question.

What had she been thinking?

But she knew. She'd wanted to shed light on her dark thoughts about ending up scarred and less whole than she was now. She'd wanted to know how McCree could still joke around and seem so unaffected by something that had caused him such pain.

Sure, his issues with his leg weren't completely analogous to her own. Still, McCree had endured a certain amount of destruction, and there was an odd comfort in knowing he'd gotten through it just fine.

He leaned back and propped his arms on the back of the bench, his jeans-clad legs long, tapering up to a torso that seemed toned even underneath the two shirts he always wore. His shoulders and chest were broad, and Jenny realized she'd never really noticed that before.

As a bolt of heat tore into places that frightened her, Jenny swallowed. Her pulse took up the rhythm and quiver of rain tapping against a closed window.

"It happened when I was in college." His voice was tight, as if this was hard for him to talk about. "I was riding my motorcycle on the way back from a cross-country meet." He caught her surprised glance and added, "Don't look so shocked. I was a long-distance runner on scholarship at the University of Kansas."

She hadn't expected this. Wasn't he more the type to hang out in the stadium parking lot instead? Wasn't he too cool for collegiate events?

"It's just…" She shook her head. "Wow, a running star."

The ghost of a smile brushed his lips, but that small change revealed so much more—a profound wistfulness. In that one instant, Jenny saw just how much he'd loved what had been taken from him. An ache dug into her chest, because she knew where this story would lead. She was so sorry for him. So sorry.

The slight smile disappeared, giving way to something haunted and maybe even a little proud. "I didn't care so much if I won, just so I got to run. I was a runner, plain and simple." He said it as if chasing the wind had been his entire reason for being; but then, probably realizing how much emotion was seeping through the pauses in his story, he continued in a matter-of-fact tone, straightening in his seat.

"Anyway, it was late, it was dark, and a car rounded

a corner, on the wrong side of the road. The driver was drunk."

She could almost see the headlights streaming through his gaze, the flare of a crash burning in his memory.

Then he blinked, shrugged.

Just like that, he was back to being the McCree she'd come to know. The mysterious flirt who used his computer—and maybe even his flippant attitude—as a wall against everyone else, even if he sat in the middle of them all the time.

"My leg got caught under the bike," he continued, "and I got dragged for quite a ways. They said I was lucky to come out of it with skin abrasions and a compound fracture. They put me in the hospital, stuck a few pins in my bones to get them back in position, and made me do some rehab."

"It allowed you to walk."

"Yeah. Walk."

He didn't have to say it. *But I don't run anymore.*

Jenny wasn't sure how to continue, so she asked, "The pins. They're still there?"

"Sure are. And so are the scars."

"And…the other driver? What happened to him or her?"

"Ah, that's the best part." McCree's grin took on a slant of the darkness she thought he'd already discarded. "A cut on the forehead. That's what he went away with."

The chilly wind picked up, moaning.

"Irony at its best," Jenny said softly, wishing she could apologize to McCree for what had happened to him. Wishing her apology wouldn't sound as meaningless as she feared it would.

He rested a hand near his leg, and she imagined what his scars might look like. How did he react when a woman saw the injured flesh during intimate moments?

She only wondered because she'd heard rumors about how many dates McCree went on. And from what she'd heard, it was a lot.

Of course, maybe the stories were only speculation from the Suds crowd, who got their information through the small-town Placid Valley grapevine.

But why was she interested in knowing?

"Still," she said, "what happened to you isn't fair."

Again, the temptation to feel sorry for herself—to wallow in how unfair *her* life might get—struck her.

Cut it out, she thought.

He was watching her by now, his light-brown eyes gauging every play of emotion across her face, just as if it were its own soap opera.

Jenny clutched her shopping bags, the plastic crumpling in her fists. Thunder protested louder now, and the market started to clear out.

"I think that might be our cue to leave," she said, standing.

"Let's go, then."

He took his time getting up, seeming stiff. Without thinking, Jenny reached out to take his computer case and shopping bag from him, just to help, but he frowned, and she knew she'd offended him.

Quickly, she dropped her hand to her side and turned around, unable to watch the rest of his mild struggle.

Instead, she lifted her face to the sky, feeling a stray drop of rain splat over her cheek.

When he limped past her, he stopped a moment, looking halfway back over his shoulder, not enough to make eye contact.

"Jenny?" he asked.

The sound of her name, so gentle, so different from the way he usually addressed her, sent a tingle up her limbs.

She rubbed her arms, chasing the sensation away.

"Yes, McCree?" she answered.

He smiled a little at the use of his last name. "I appreciate the thought."

Then he moved on.

She waited for a moment, wondering where she stood with him now that she'd heard his story, then caught up to him.

They walked slowly to the corner.

"What did you do after the accident?" she asked. "You probably couldn't keep your scholarship."

He didn't seem fazed. "Right. I lost it, and I couldn't afford to stay in school. But I knew I was good at computers, so I studied, learned on my own, did some freelance work with software that earned me some nice bucks. Then I came out here eventually, and now I'm putting it all together into my own business."

Had he also created an aggressive sense of humor after the accident? While he was abandoning his old home for someplace where no one knew him? And was his humor a way for him to direct attention away from his injury?

She wondered how she would end up coping....

Pushing aside the thought, she smiled, wanting so badly to inject some levity into their conversation. "So you left Kansas, just like Dorothy and Toto."

"But without the tornado. In case you couldn't guess, I was kind of restless, and Northern California appealed to me. San Francisco, Haight-Ashbury—it seemed like my kind of place."

They stopped at the last crosswalk before her apartment complex, and she glanced at his slight goatee, his longish, ruffled hair. He definitely wasn't a hippie, but he had a freewheeling style that went well with his new home.

McCree obviously sensed her perusal, because he volleyed his own right back at her, scanning her cheekily, no doubt just to give as good as he'd gotten.

His gaze started at her tennis-shoed feet, traveled up her legs…

Jenny's flesh began a slow burn, shooting heat into the pit of her belly, where it radiated until she was holding her breath at the swell of it. For one taboo moment, she clung to the sensation. It'd been so long since she'd been with a man, so long since she'd felt this way….

But as McCree's gaze coasted up to her chest, her confidence guttered, snuffed out. She folded her arms over her breasts, careful not to come into much contact with the left one.

McCree's grin disappeared; in fact, he seemed apologetic for being so forward.

The light turned green, and she entered the crosswalk, grateful for the reprieve.

How could he be looking at her that way when she was wearing these clothes? Didn't he have eyes?

Yet even as she asked the questions, a latent glow consumed Jenny.

He'd acted as if she were still appealing.

And maybe that scared her even more. She couldn't be attractive, because being with a man would only complicate what she might have to deal with in these coming months…or, even in the coming *years*.

As it started to sprinkle, they arrived at her apartment complex—a clean-lined, gray brick structure with an iron gate blocking the entry courtyard. She fished in her jacket pocket for the key.

The rain turned from a sprinkle to a heavier shower that clicked on the awning that covered them.

"You have an umbrella?" Jenny asked, eyeing his computer case. She doubted he cared much about his hair and clothing getting wet.

"Me?" he asked. "What, do I look like Gene Kelly to you?"

"I take that as a no." She took out her key and inserted it into the lock. "I've got one at my place if you need it."

He held a hand to his heart, as if overwhelmed. "Imagine that. I get to catch a peek of Jenny Hunter's apartment. Please, tell me this isn't just a tease."

Panic flashed red in her mind's eye.

McCree?

Hovering in her doorway?

Then again, a decent person would invite him *inside,* just until the rain let up.

Shoot.

"Don't look so horrified. I'm just yanking your chain." He nodded in the direction of the Suds Club, and lightning lit the sky, followed by a laugh of thunder. "My place really isn't that far."

Shoot, shoot, shoot.

He'd walked Jenny to her door and here she was, having to compose a mental thesis about why she shouldn't invite him in. When had she gotten to be so standoffish?

Well, it wasn't as if having him inside for a snack would be the same as letting him slip an engagement ring on her finger or anything.

She pushed the gate open just as the sky really opened up with a gush of rain that pounded on the overhang. Covering her resignation with a polite expression, she pointed at a first-floor door that led to her town house. They could reach it by walking under a cover of foliage that wouldn't let through too much rain.

When they got to her door, she unlocked it, then flung it open and gestured to him to enter the tiled foyer before her.

Company was company, after all.

Afterward, she sent a nasty look to the sky, but it only taunted her with more rain, clapping on the ground like gleeful applause.

A half hour later, Liam sat on Jenny's plush velvet couch, leaning back and waiting for his mug of hot green tea to cool. She'd been kind enough to make it for him just after he'd been asked to doff his rough, work-type boots on a thick woven mat by the door.

She was in the kitchen—a room that opened to the common area, so he could see her at the stove. The curry-and-ginger aroma of her moong dal recipe floated to him; she was using her farmers' market purchases to whip up an afternoon snack as the rain chattered outside.

Earlier, when he'd told her about the accident, he'd read the sympathy on her face, and it had felt…well, not bad. He wasn't sure what he'd expected from Jenny—disgust at knowing he wasn't perfect?

Or did that only happen when he showed his leg to a woman?

He shoved away the thought. Telling her hadn't been as hard as he'd envisioned. As a matter of fact, it'd lifted a weight off his chest, making the words come easy and honest.

Who knew?

Of course, that didn't mean he'd be as free with his story to anyone else.

"I thought you said you couldn't cook." He shifted on the couch so he could face her, and even though the motion set his leg hurting again, he'd be damned if he showed that it bothered him. He'd been mortified enough at the market, and he'd bite back every twist of pain for the rest of the day if he had to.

In the kitchen, Jenny was spooning her creation out of a pot and into a bowl. "When did I say I couldn't cook?"

"At the Laundromat today."

She sent him a curious glance, as if wondering what else he'd heard from his corner.

Uh-oh.

He tried to seem harmless, as if he didn't know her big secret. "Of course," he added, "there's always a chance that I misheard you."

"No, you didn't."

She grabbed some beige ceramic bowls and brought them out of the kitchen, positioning them on two yarn-dyed place mats she'd already put on the low, glass-topped table in front of the couch. She added spoons and a plate of the pumpkin-stuffed paratha bread to the settings.

"As a single girl," she said, "I just don't cook much, so I'm out of practice. Cooking usually means big portions that I have to eat for leftovers, and I like variety. Besides, who has the time?"

He wondered what else she didn't have time for—boyfriends? Lately, Jenny never seemed to have any dating news to share—not as far as he could tell from Suds gossip.

"So you're 'out of practice,'" he said, tearing off a piece of the paratha and sampling it. Not bad. Not bad at all. "Were you ever *in* practice with cooking?"

While she went back to the kitchen to retrieve a bigger, matching bowl containing the moong dal con-coction, she nodded.

"When I was younger—high school—I decided I'd take it upon myself to become the family chef on Sundays. I'd pore over my mom's cookbooks, pick out something cool like Steak Diane, then go for it. I suppose I did pretty well, too."

She returned, putting the big bowl on yet another place mat. The contents resembled bumpy, hot pudding, but he didn't comment as she went back to the kitchen one more time to fetch them two glasses of water before she finally sat down.

But even seated, she stayed busy, spooning the food into his bowl, then hers. "I cooked for the family during the week sometimes, too, but nothing as grand. My mom helped Dad with farming chores, so I did what I could between my homework and housework."

Liam took the small bowl she'd proffered, breathing in the exotic steam. Smelled pretty good. Spicy and earthy.

"Farming, huh?" he asked.

Just as she obviously hadn't expected him to be on the cross-country team, he hadn't expected to hear that Jenny Hunter was anything but a born-and-raised city girl.

"My parents owned a walnut grove in Visalia," she said, naming a small town almost four hours southeast of Placid Valley. "I'm an only child, so there was always work to be done, especially since Mom and Dad also held day jobs."

Liam settled back against the couch. "Well, what do you know. And here I thought I was the provincial one in this room."

"Kansas and Visalia..." She stirred her snack with a spoon. "Maybe we do have something in common."

She went still for a moment, and he knew the exact reason. She was thinking about his leg, her possible cancer, and how they could have something in common there, too, as wounded people.

Silent, they both tasted the dish at the same time, and when he nodded in appreciation of the slightly spicy food, she smiled.

"Lentils are supposed to be really good for you," she said, taking another bite.

He almost asked if she planned on changing her diet to hard-core health food stuff like this from now on, but he took a drink of water instead. Keeping this secret of hers wasn't easy, especially when just about everything she said reminded him of the doubts and fears she must've been battling. All he could do was say the right things.

And that was all he should do.

He put down his glass while she reached for hers, and their hands brushed.

They jerked back from each other, a current zapping up his arm and shooting straight into his gut. Desire melted lower, into his groin, as all his fantasies about her exploded into a pulsing flash that covered his vision.

Her lips on his mouth…

Her fingers working at his shirt, teasing him with a hint of what was to come…

When he shook himself out of it, Jenny was sitting on the edge of her seat and drinking her water as if nothing had happened. Finished, she let out an exhalation.

"Whoo, this recipe has got some kick to it. More than I'm used to, anyway."

She was totally ignoring their contact. The explosion that had apparently rocked him and him alone.

He'd heard people say, "My heart sank," but he'd never really known the true meaning of it until now. His attraction to her was as one-sided as ever.

Shoving more moong dal into his mouth, he made sure he couldn't say anything—not until he collected himself.

Afterward, he set the bowl on the place mat.

The rain was still beating on the windows, and he

didn't want to go out in it. Normally, he would've just stayed in the Laundromat until the skies allowed him a break to head home, but he'd impulsively wanted to catch up with Jenny instead. Now he reconsidered.

Maybe he should go ahead and grab that spare umbrella of hers and scoot on out of here....

Jenny got up from her chair, reminding him of a Jill-in-the-box. She was that high-strung.

Wasn't that a good sign, though? Didn't it mean she was aware of some sexual tension?

She grabbed all the bowls and took them to the kitchen sink, where she rinsed them out.

"Can I help with anything?" Liam asked.

"I've got it all covered, thanks."

The water splashed against stainless steel.

Did she want him gone now? Damn, he needed to ask for that umbrella.

She finished all too quickly, then came back out, drying her hands. Had she ever been this hyper around her friends at the Club?

No, Jenny had always been so polished, so together.

Without warning, she started laughing. Laughing so hard that she had to lean against the wall.

Liam wasn't sure if he should be laughing, too.

Then she caught a breath, shook her head. "Sorry. This is just so...so surreal. Me and you alone in the same room, outside of the Laundromat. If anyone saw us now, they wouldn't recognize us."

He got it, and it was funny, even though he wasn't laughing himself. When he'd woken up this morning, the last thing he would've expected was to be spending a couple hours with her. And if anyone had told him that he and Jenny Hunter would engage in a serious talk on the way home from the Suds Club and that he would be sitting on a couch in her apartment…

Her laughter tapering off, Jenny dabbed at her eyes with the hand towel, then tossed it into the kitchen, where it landed on a counter.

"I'm not really sure what I should be saying to you, what we should be talking about."

"What would you talk to anyone about?"

Her laughter faded altogether, and she wiped her eyes again.

"I don't know anymore," she said softly.

Her words were so loaded that he couldn't do anything but look down, fearing she might see the truth on his face. If she realized that he'd indeed overheard her conversation with Mei, things would definitely change. He didn't know her well enough for it to be his business, and he guessed that she might feel invaded somehow. She hadn't chosen to tell him, after all, and he suspected a woman like her valued always having a choice.

He decided to face their tension head-on. "We're not comfortable around each other. Alone."

She bit her bottom lip and, out of what seemed to be a new habit that made all too much sense in light of her secret, she pulled her baggy shirt away from her chest.

"It's too bad I make you uncomfortable," he added.

"Oh, you don't." She stopped messing with her shirt. "Okay, maybe you do. I guess I'm just so used to hearing you kid around all the time. You know—the guy in the back of the Suds Club who makes light of the soap opera in the hope that no one will guess that he's actually really into it."

"I hide it that well, huh?"

Their gazes met, and it seemed they both knew that she'd deftly maneuvered the conversation away from their "discomfort" with each other to a safer place.

But what did he expect? A woman like Jenny was out of his league.

The rain had tapered off, so he slowly stood and grabbed his mug, then took it to the sink. "Well, thanks for entertaining me. My nice-and-dry computer thanks you, too."

"No problem. My rusty cooking skills appreciated the practice."

She sounded just as relieved as he was, and he couldn't help hating that.

He wanted her to want him here.

"Your cooking's great, Jenny," he said. "Really…great."

In spite of himself, his words were laden with something beyond a mere compliment. All of his yearning was out there, ready for the next heartbeat, the next strained intake of breath.

All he had to do was say what he was really feeling.

I want you, Jenny. I always have, and I always will, no matter what.

But saying it would only guarantee a replay of every failed relationship he'd attempted. He might make her happy for a month, but when it came time to go deeper, he would come up lacking, because he could never be what he used to be—free and whole.

And he could never forget it.

Her eyes were wide, as if she expected him to go on. As if she were terrified by the possibility that he would.

Relating to that, Liam merely held up a hand in a silent goodbye, donned his boots and grabbed his computer and shopping bag. Then he left Jenny's place, a dull ache in his chest because he wished he could tell her how he really felt.

Chapter Four

Jenny's office, which overlooked the San Francisco financial district, could barely hold her corporation-issued desk, much less a potted palm and the set of oaken shelves where she neatly filed her project folders.

But squeeze in four co-workers who were Monday-morning-quarterbacking yesterday's 49ers game and there was wall-to-wall chaos.

It didn't help that she could hardly keep her mind on the project at hand, anyway, even days after McCree had opened up to her with the story about how he'd injured his leg. And it wasn't so much that she kept thinking about what he'd told her as that she kept wondering what else the mystery guy was hiding about himself. What else lay beneath the facade that didn't seem quite so careless now.

She struggled to stay on task, but she kept seeing

Liam's compassionate brown gaze, kept sinking into this new, fluttering awareness that'd slammed her just when the last thing she needed to be doing was thinking about him....

Her team partner, Bryan Teague, broke into her thoughts with the football chatter.

"Fourth down and less than a yard to go on the fifty," he said while sitting next to Jenny at her desk, supposedly brainstorming ideas for the Thayer account. "And what do we do? Punt the ball. It'll be a miracle if we even get to the playoffs with conservative play calling like that."

Jenny emphatically drew a large circle in the middle of a yellow legal pad, just to get Bryan back on the task of coming up with a marketing angle for the Thayer Closet Butler, a device that was part organizing revolving rack with legions of compartments and part computerized personal assistant that kept track of what was stored where.

She tapped the paper with her pencil eraser to refocus Bryan's attention. "Coach had faith that our defense would hold their offense for the rest of the game, so why take needless chances when we were ahead?"

Then she wrote the word Butler in the middle of the circle.

But when her other three co-workers—who weren't even on the Thayer account—continued to break down the game, Jenny caught Bryan's eye.

He got the message, then got serious, talking over the other guys as he threw out a comment to begin their marketing brainstorm.

"Having a butler means that a person doesn't have to do as much work themselves," he said.

"Having a butler," Jenny added, "means someone else—or something else, in this case—does the work for you. The Closet Butler takes care of the small stuff so you don't have to. And you don't even have to take care of him."

Suddenly, the football talk stopped, and Jenny raised her head from the powwow. There, in her doorway, stood the boss—Mr. Pete Findley—in all his straight-tied, slicked-back golden-haired glory. He glanced around as the other men stared into their coffee mugs and shoved their hands into their pockets.

"Am I missing a meeting?" Findley asked, addressing all of them in a baritone that he used to great advantage.

"We're just brainstorming for the Butler," Jenny said, smiling affably.

Ever since Findley had taken charge last year, they'd all been busting their butts to impress him, but it wasn't easy. Even a nod of approval from the boss was a bonus, especially these days, when work seemed to be one of the only things that made Jenny think she could transcend what was going on in her personal life. That it could even help her to shine in other areas so no one would have to look too closely at her physically.

The thought reminded her of McCree and how she'd wondered if he used his sense of humor to hide the pain of his own injuries.

McCree, McCree, McCree. Why did everything always come back around to him lately?

When her partner Bryan cleared his throat, Jenny sat straighter, forcing herself to forget Liam McCree.

Good thing, too, because Findley was giving everyone in the room their own we'll-see-what-your-numbers-say-at-the-end-of-the-week glance.

He ended on the three stooges still standing near the door and holding their coffee mugs.

"Looking forward to our progress meetings, then," Findley said. Her trio of co-workers nodded as the boss lasered in on Jenny now.

"Hunter, can I have a word with you in my office?"

He moved out, leaving the others to stay quiet while she rose from her seat to follow him, her heart in her throat.

Being called to "the office" wasn't usually a great sign, but it had happened to all her co-workers at one time or another. And she was pretty sure this wasn't about a raise, either, since Findley gave them only on a well-established merit and seniority scale, and she wasn't due for a couple of months.

Yet she pretty much knew what this was about: her recent uncleared absences.

As she got to the door, Bryan quietly said, "Give him hell for me."

The other guys agreed and she grinned at them, even though, inside, she was a mess of anxiety. She took such pride in doing well here, and yes, she had chosen to keep the truth of her absences to herself, but she was back to form now that the shock of last week's news had almost worn off. Maybe it hadn't completely disappeared, but a few days—and McCree's story about having bounced back from his own loss—had at least given her perspective enough to think that she'd be able to face whatever punches might be in store for her.

Still, a weight sat in her stomach as she entered Findley's leather-and-brass domain, then shut the door behind her. She kept cool as he motioned to a chair in front of the desk where he was sitting. She noticed the pictures he displayed of his family: a pearls-and-linen-wearing wife, two wide-eyed kids. Findley was a person, she told herself.

No need to fear him.

"Morning, Jennifer," he said, picking up a pen and opening a ledger. "How was your weekend?"

Not as great as usual, she thought. Unless she counted Friday, when she'd been able to escape a little at the farmers' market with McCree.

Concentrate. "It went well, Pete. How about yours?"

"Well enough, thank you. And the Thayer account? What's the status?"

Right to business, but that was why he was the boss. "We're honing a slogan."

He scribbled something in that ledger, and Jenny was reminded of a psychoanalyst tearing apart each nuance of a patient's answer.

"The presentation for the client," he continued. "It'll be ready next week, as scheduled?"

"Absolutely."

"Good. I'm having lunch with their CEO soon." More scribbles, but he talked while he wrote now. "I've had my concerns, Jennifer. That's why I'm asking."

It was as if he'd shot at her and hit the center of the target.

She *wanted* to do well. Couldn't he see that?

"We're on track, Pete," she repeated.

He put down his pen, closed the ledger. "You know that I run a tight ship, and that I have definite ideas about what kind of employee works in bringing a business from one level to the next."

She launched a preemptory strike. "I worked from home all weekend to make up for lost time. Believe me, I'm not slacking off."

"But here's the issue." He leaned his arms on his desk, clasping his hands. "If I make excuses for one employee about company policy, I need to do it for the next, and I can't do that. You have two write-ups now, Jennifer, and you've only got one left. Do you understand?"

She nodded, but at the same time, a tiny voice in the back of her head was saying, *He's just counseling me. I've worked hard at this job. I...*

She gripped her skirt in a fist.

I am this job right now.

Her career had come to mean even more than she'd thought. Truthfully, when she was here, there was usually no time for thinking about what-ifs in the outside, more personal world. Here, she could lose herself in ideas for most of the day and face her other reality only when she finally decided to go home.

She leaned forward in her chair, hoping her desperation wasn't obvious. "I understand, Pete."

"Okay. It's only that you're on thin ice. Taking care of life shouldn't be a problem, because, like the other employees, you already have one day a week to work from home, and the company has been pretty magnanimous in giving that to you. You've been gone a lot." He furrowed his brow. "Is there something going on, Jennifer? Something we should…talk about?"

Her defenses rose. She wasn't going to allow the lump to chip away at this part of her life, too—the one part she had more control of.

"There's nothing to talk about," she said. "Just a few unexpected sick days that came up."

He seemed relieved. "Good. It's good to know you've recovered."

But even as he said it, panic set in.

She'd scheduled her biopsy for next Wednesday, at the first open time that wouldn't conflict with work hours, but…

What if?

What if she ended up having to go through treatments that made her ill? She'd have to be that sick girl instead of the office top dog, and the prospect chipped away at her world.

She cleared her throat, making sure her voice wasn't going to quaver as she looked him in the eyes. "As always, I'll put *everything* I have into this job, Pete. Everything."

"Thank you, Jennifer."

It looked as if he wanted to ask her something else, but he went back to his ledger, becoming the company man once again.

When she closed the door behind her, she exhaled.

But when she went back to an office that had emptied in her absence, she was drawn more to her window— where the sky was a cloudless blue—than to her work.

She touched the glass, smiling as she thought of how

the breeze had felt on her face last week, when Liam McCree had provided her with the first breath of air she'd felt in a while.

Liam set his computer on his plastic chair, then moved several feet away to get the scope of the home page he'd designed for his fledgling business.

He assessed his design—sleek, professional, straightforward.

Pretty damned good.

Yet it didn't have any…

Well, *zing*.

As always, he thought of Jenny and her creativity, her savvy. He'd heard her talk to friends in the Club about her job, and she was always so animated when she explained an idea she was working on. He knew without a doubt that she was someone who understood *zing*.

His blood warmed just at the thought of her. God, he wished it were Wednesday—her day to come to the Club. The room seemed a lot emptier without her here.

"Why so thoughtful, McCree?" Mei Webb asked as she approached the bank of dryers near him while holding a basket of damp wash to her side. Pink clothing for her four-year-old seemed to make up most of the pile.

"Just going over a job," he said, gesturing to his computer. His instincts voted to shut the laptop so he could keep his life private, just as he normally did when someone tried to get too close. He'd learned how to do that after the accident, when he'd discovered that most people didn't like to look at uncovered scars on legs— or mental scars under the surface.

His standoffish personality often came in handy.

No doubt sensing Liam's protectiveness, Mei smiled without glancing at his computer, then loaded her clothing into a dryer, her long black hair spilling over part of her face.

Since she'd reconciled with her husband, Travis, she'd been all smiles, and it was nice to see. Not that Liam had any emotional investment in the reunion whatsoever, but…

Okay, maybe he had been rooting for them to work things out, based on the conversations he'd picked up between her and Jenny in the Club. He had a heart, after all, even if the women he'd dated might testify to the contrary.

But, in his defense, he did tend to break things off before a partner could come to any conclusions about him.

He realized that Mei was actually peeking through her hair to catch a glimpse of what was on his computer screen.

Ah, what the hell. He'd told Jenny about his accident, and that hadn't done him in. Why not bow to something way less significant like this?

After Mei finished loading her clothes, he turned the chair in her direction, and she slowly closed the dryer, as if stunned that he was allowing her in, even just a tad.

"This isn't the final version of my site," he said. "Not yet."

"That's gorgeous." She came closer. "You've got a good eye for design."

He didn't tell her that he still wasn't happy with it, that it still wasn't "there."

"Business consulting, huh?" she asked.

"With an emphasis in online growth. I took a few

classes in marketing during my college days, but more important, I worked for an uncle after…"

His words trailed off as he thought of the accident. When he'd told Jenny, she'd gotten sympathetic on him. But Liam didn't do well with sympathy. He'd only allowed it from her because of what she was going through. Right…?

He continued, deciding to skip to the easier part with Mei. "I worked freelance for my uncle after college. He put me through some trial by fire in the business field, but I'm hoping to hire a marketing genius to partner with me in the near future to double what I have to offer."

"You know, I've had some ideas for Baby Boom-Boom. Maybe I could talk to you sometime about them? On a professional level, of course."

He nodded, knowing that she had a burgeoning online baby-clothing store. "I'm always in the office."

She laughed, leaning against the dryers. "So when you tease Jenny about coming on board with you, it's no joke."

"No joke at all." It stung to realize that Mei had doubted his intentions. But who could blame her when he hardly seemed like the business type?

Maybe, along with his Web site, he'd need a makeover.

Mei pulled up another plastic chair so she could sit and give his work a closer gander, but when she spoke, she did it in a too-offhanded way that told him she wasn't really being so casual.

"Jenny told me that you two had some quality time in her apartment the other day," she said.

The memory sent a thrill through him. "She was kind enough to welcome a guy in out of the rain."

Mei slid him a glance. "She seemed to be doing a lot better after your talk with her, Liam."

He crossed his arms over his chest, strictly out of habit. His feelings about Jenny were nothing to fool with, even though he hoped to God he looked like he couldn't care less.

"What I mean," Mei continued, "is that…"

She obviously wasn't sure how to finish.

"Let me guess," he said. "Based on how Jenny had a ten-mile stare last week, she could use all the under-standing she can get right now for whatever she's going through. And I happened to provide some at the right time."

"Exactly."

"How's she doing?" he asked in spite of all the red alerts going through him to stay the hell out of it.

But maybe it was already too late.

"She's a trouper," Mei said. She was being cautious about revealing too much, and he knew it was because she wasn't about to tell him the secret Jenny had so carefully entrusted to her. But from the way she was watching him, he could tell that she highly suspected he knew more than he should.

"Glad to hear it," he said. "I'm not used to seeing her without all that verve."

"None of us are." She gave Liam a look that he didn't quite know how to interpret.

Unless…

My God, was he wearing his heart on his damned sleeve? Could Mei tell how he felt about Jenny, even though he'd been doing his best to hide it?

When she smiled at him again—an encouraging smile—he panicked a little, feeling as if a portion of himself was open to harm now.

A flash of memory overcame him: a woman who'd gotten too close to him when they were both in their midtwenties, when he'd just been teaching himself how to cope with the scars. One night he'd shown them to her, and her face...

Her face.

She'd tried to pretend that the sight of his damage didn't matter, but there'd been that moment of revelation that she could never take back.

From then on, he'd been far more careful, never involving emotions. He didn't get hurt that way.

Mei finally spoke, reaching out to pat his arm. "It's really nice that you care."

"Yeah."

What a relief—she didn't know how he ached for Jenny, how he couldn't stop thinking about her night after night.

He'd made too much out of nothing.

And when she walked away, Liam couldn't help feeling incredibly relieved that his emotions were going to stay under wraps, where they were most comfortable.

The past couple of days, Jenny had put more than even the usual amount of labor into the Thayer account's upcoming presentation, even waking up and starting her office hours at four in the morning on work-from-home Wednesday. So by the time lunch came around, she was ready to emerge from her cave for a well-earned break.

She put on her iPod and walked around the neighborhood to combat her early wake-up by taking in some fresh air, then made her way to the Suds Club for an hour of *Flamingo Beach* and companionship.

But when she entered the Laundromat, the last thing she expected was to find herself checking out McCree's corner before looking anywhere else.

The second-to-last thing she expected was to discover him sitting up a little straighter in his chair when he saw her.

As they snagged gazes, everything seemed to suspend—the sound of the bell on the door, the welcomes from the other women, time itself. Her heart even seemed to float as oxygen deserted her.

Yet the second his lips melted into a slow smile, everything pounded back into motion, the room bursting into sound and color.

Jenny found that she was smiling at him, too.

Was it because he'd sensed something was wrong with her and he'd treated her so kindly when she'd needed it the most last week? Or was it because she was still being too emotional and it was affecting her judgment now?

After all, she couldn't be dependent on someone else when she needed to develop her own strength first.

She made herself glance away from him and wave to everyone else while she took out her earbuds. Then she wandered toward the television.

In her peripheral vision, she couldn't help noticing that McCree had shut the top of his computer, set the machine down on his chair, then stood.

Her stomach flipped. Was he coming over to say hi?

And why was her body starting to get kind of tingly about that?

Be rational, she thought. *It's just McCree, Jenny.*

She made her way over to the viewing area, intending to say hi to him on the way and then get back to normal. Whatever that was.

"Hey," she said as she came within several feet of him.

"Hi," he said.

She caught his scent: something like cedar. Woodsy. Fresh.

Yum.

And, this close, she realized again how tall he was and how that appealed to her. She'd always liked men who had some height.

He was watching her with a glimmer in his gaze, as if he truly was glad to see her but was playing it down.

Her heart started thudding again, especially when he jerked his chin toward her iPod in a silent question. She understood that he was asking what she was listening to.

"I downloaded an audiobook," she said. "I haven't had a lot of time to read, but I can listen while I walk. Each year, I forget how beautiful autumn walks are."

"So you're multitasking, like any good businessperson."

She smiled at the compliment; it was nice to hear after having been so on her toes with the boss lately. "Actually, I'm not listening to anything that'll get me ahead in my career. It's more…"

She shrugged.

"What?" he asked softly.

Oh, God, his voice. He sounded like he really cared what she was listening to.

She answered without giving him a hard time; after their honest discussions, it seemed the most natural thing in the world to do now.

"I'm listening to a story about a woman who sets out to discover some meaning in her life," she said, hoping her choice of book wasn't too telling. "The author went to Italy, India and Indonesia, and she has this really peaceful way of relating what she found in each place. It's inspirational."

She didn't mention that the author also had a peaceful way of making her think that everything could turn out for the best if she could take her life in hand and refuse to allow all the what-ifs to control her.

McCree had gotten a faraway look in his eyes, along with a little smile on his lips.

"Italy," he said.

"You say it like you've been there."

"A long time ago." He raised an eyebrow and stroked the small patch of hair on his chin.

"Something happen in Italy that you'd like to share?"

He moved away from the dryers, his smile cryptic.

"Misspent youth?" she asked, pursuing the subject on impulse. Or maybe because she really did want to know. "A troublemaking summer?"

"Okay, okay."

He glanced around, then lowered his voice, as if he knew she was going to get him to tell her anyway, so why not make the process easier?

"Early in college," he said, "some deep-pocketed supporters of the athletic department thought it might be interesting to unofficially send some of us kids to a marathon in Rome. It was a cultural experience for us, they said, but I think they wanted to show us off, too. We had a real good crop of athletes that year."

"And did you do them proud?"

"During the race? Definitely. After the race?" He grinned.

"McCree," she said, a laugh bubbling from just behind her words.

Suddenly, he looked really content, and she wondered if it was because he'd gotten her to cheer up again. She didn't know how to react. She had that kind of influence on someone?

"Well," he said, "let's just say there was a gathering at the hotel and a long night of exploring the ins and outs of the city."

This time she didn't hold back her laughter, because she could imagine just what a rascal he must've been.

He smiled, and she realized that he was listening to her, enjoying her mirth.

Such a small thing to appreciate—laughter. And she hadn't experienced enough of it lately.

"Jenny!" someone called out from the seats.

She turned around, discovering that they had a crowd of seven women watching them. One, Charlotte, was motioning her to come over and sit. Mei wasn't here today, but Jenny suspected she would've been doing the same.

In back of her, McCree spoke. "They'd really love it if you just graced them with your presence, Jenny."

Jenny.

She liked how her name sounded when he said it.

Before she knew it, she was doing something she'd never anticipated doing in a hundred years.

"Why don't you sit with us, McCree?"

He'd obviously never anticipated that, either. In a gesture that clearly asked, "Me?", he pointed to his chest.

That broad chest.

She couldn't take her eyes off it for a second, but then she recovered, except for the telltale thumping of her pulse.

"Yeah," she said, her voice so quiet she barely recognized it. "You."

Their gazes linked once again, drawn, magnetized, as she felt the pull of him.

"Jenny!" Charlotte repeated.

She blinked, started to move toward the group, but then she inclined her head in a second invitation to McCree. He glanced at his corner, with the computer waiting there for him, and she remembered that the laptop was more than just his business. It was something like a shield, too. A barrier that he'd erected, even in the middle of a crowd.

But why would he do that? she wondered. She knew he had to be more social outside of the Club, with all those rumored dates, and probably even friends....

Didn't he have friends?

Her heart broke a bit at the question, and without thinking, she grabbed his shirt and tugged at the hem, pulling him along with her to the seats.

When the women by the TV saw McCree away from his normal spot, they cheered Jenny on.

"Catch of the day!" a woman named Vivian yelled.

They went to the back row of chairs, with Jenny leading him to a seat on the end, just to give him an out in case he changed his mind and wanted to go back to the way things had been before. Lord knew from the way he was shaking his head at the teasing women as he sat, he might need to make an escape. As peace of mind for her own benefit, Jenny also left a chair open between herself and McCree. Space, she thought. A sign that she wasn't plotting any further intimacy with him. That this was as far as anything would go between them.

After the victory of finally getting McCree into the center of the room, the women focused on the TV, where *Flamingo Beach* was getting into full swing with Trina and Dash's interrupted wedding. And while Jenny watched the program, she crossed one leg over the other, anchoring her hand on the empty chair that separated her and McCree. He'd slumped down into his own seat, his booted ankle resting on his thigh, which made his knee hover over the in-between chair, too.

So close, Jenny thought, looking at how his jeans molded to the lean muscles of his leg. Something naughty in her wanted to touch him, to see how he would feel in the weathered denim.

She'd gone a long time without actually making love to a man—not since she and Franklin, her most serious boyfriend, had broken up.

My God. She'd dated enough, but she hadn't connected with anyone since then. She started to yearn for it, mostly because she wondered when she would allow herself to be open on such an intimate level again.

McCree seemed to sense her thoughts—or maybe just the fall of her posture—and he glanced over. Then, before she could react, he cupped his hand over the one she was resting on that seat between them, as if to assure her everything would be all right.

Her skin came alive, warm, sensitized under his palm. But just as the vibrations traveled up her arm and blazed out through her chest in piercing heat, he squeezed her hand and removed his own.

Leaving her skin crying out for him to touch her again.

Chapter Five

Even an hour later, after *Flamingo Beach* had ended and Liam had gotten out of his chair, grumbling about silly soap weddings just to get the goat of the women around him, he still felt Jenny's hand beneath his palm.

And in the very center of him, too.

Good God, he'd just touched her hand, and here he was, acting as if the earth had shifted beneath his feet. But no matter how hard he tried to play off the quake of the innocent contact, he couldn't.

He couldn't stop denying that no one had ever moved him like this, and that frightened him to damned death, because he hadn't proven to be of much use to any woman before.

Why would Jenny be any different?

So he left her by the TV with a casual goodbye, then

went back to his corner by the dryers, thinking how much more comfortable it was there. But upon reflection, he decided to pack up for the day and finish work at his apartment. It'd been restlessness that had goaded him to take up the Suds Club as his office in the first place. Now his acute awareness of Jenny—and the certainty that he needed to go while the going was good—made him think that being closed in by his own walls might be a better feeling than the one he was experiencing right now.

As he headed for the exit, the women called to him, as if he were one of their crowd now. A poke of what he thought might be acceptance got to him before he drove it out and merely held up his hand in farewell instead.

Yet a grin snuck up on him, too, and he barely got out the exit before they could see it.

As he closed the door, he suddenly found Jenny right behind him, and his pulse pistoned.

She was wearing that oversized yellow jacket again, her hair pulled back from a freshly scrubbed face, sans the makeup she'd always worn before. But she didn't have to be fashionable to do crazy things to his heart.

"That was the best wedding in years," she said, matching him step for step on the sidewalk.

"It was a fictional wedding."

"But sweet all the same, especially when Delia got locked in that closet and couldn't cause any more trouble for Dash and Trina. I love a nice show of karma."

They passed a drugstore, then a shoe boutique. Up ahead, he could smell the fresh bread and garlic from Amati's, a small Italian restaurant where he often ate dinner after putting in a day at the Club. But over it all, he breathed in Jenny's scent, a clover essence from her shampoo or bath gel. It spun his mind, just like a fast run would've done so long ago.

"Do you remember when Hart and Julianna were on the soap?" she added, referring to one of *Flamingo Beach*'s most popular star-crossed couples. "Now, that was a wedding, too. Or maybe that was before your time."

His senses were still in too much of an uproar for him to answer. Was she still feeling his hand on hers, as well?

He could imagine just how it'd go down if he asked her. *Hey, Jenny, you know how I touched you earlier? Well, it rocked my world, even though you probably don't even recall it happening.*

Better to keep her as an ideal than something he'd end up ruining with his inability to commit, he thought. Better to just keep his mouth shut and suffer his feelings silently until they ran their course. Because they would.

Even if he didn't remember ever feeling quite this strongly before.

"I'm not a new fan of the soap," he finally said as he stepped aside so a woman with a stroller could pass on the narrow walkway. "I've been tuned in since I was a teenager, when my mom would tape *Flamingo Beach* and watch it after she got home from work."

"Well, well," Jenny said, and he almost thought there was something like admiration in her tone. "You're secure enough to admit that you're not just in the laundry to do your clothes and conduct business."

"Might as well come clean." At least about the small stuff.

At Amati's, which was merely yards away now, he could hear the wild laughter of children, and when two dark-headed boys darted out of the restaurant and into the café table section out front, Liam smiled. Michael and Anthony Amati were chasing each other around again.

Liam had always wondered what it might be like to have a brother. Or to be an uncle. He even wondered if he would've made a great father if life had gone differently.

As he and Jenny arrived in front of the restaurant, the boys dashed out from behind the black iron fencing and right in front of them, with Michael getting ready to fire an onion at Anthony.

"Whoa, whoa," Liam said, automatically taking a step in front of Jenny and using his computer case to block her from any flying debris that might result from a direct hit to the younger boy's back. "I thought your parents got on you about having these food wars. Remember not too long ago when you hit Dave Chandler with that tomato?"

"We're more careful now," Michael said, hiding the onion behind his back. The younger one, Anthony, offered a big smile, complete with a missing front tooth. Their big chocolate eyes were filled with an innocence Liam sincerely doubted yet fell for anyway.

Jenny stepped out from behind Liam, and when she gave him an amused glance, he realized what he'd done: shielded her like some sort of onion-fighting white knight come to the rescue.

Thing was, he had no doubt Jenny could rescue herself if she had a mind to.

He gave her some room by stepping away from her,

but not before he saw her grin in clear appreciation of his so-called chivalry.

Liam shrugged, unwilling to take such credit. It wasn't as if he'd flown in front of a bullet. Still, the warm flow of being recognized like that lingered.

When a woman in her early twenties rushed out the door to scold the boys, Liam nodded to her in greeting. She resembled Michael and Anthony with her liquid brown eyes and olive skin, and as she herded her brothers back behind the iron fence, she touched her hair, which was falling out of its bun, as if thinking she was a mess.

"Hi, Liam," she said. "Please tell me these dervishes didn't get you."

"No harm done, Sophia," he said.

"Thank goodness." She rattled off a string of Italian to the boys, who nodded and looked like tiny angels who could never possibly get into any trouble. When she was done, Michael plopped the onion into Sophia's outstretched palm and led Anthony by the hand over to Liam.

"Sorry," they said in stereo, wearing dorky yet endearing grins.

"It's okay this time, guys," he said.

He didn't have it in him to scold more than that, so he ruffled their hair and sent them on their way.

But the boys only giggled, then hung around to stare up at him for some reason. Maybe because he usually joked around with the kids when he came by for a meal. Maybe because they liked to hear the dumb stories he told them about his childhood in Kansas, like the time when he was seven and he'd climbed up a neighbor's windmill, only to have to wait for the fire department to help him back down when the ladder broke on his return trip. It'd been meant as a cautionary tale, but Liam thought the Amati boys might've construed it as something adventurous instead.

Jenny's laughter filtered into his consciousness, and when he glanced at her, he was taken off guard by how she was watching him and the boys as if she thought it was cute that they worshipped him. He'd need to explain that this wasn't some magic touch he had. Kids weren't in his future.

But when she glanced back at the boys and her gaze took a turn for the dimmer, he wondered if she'd started thinking about *her* future again.

Had Jenny ever wanted to have a family and children? Had her lump made her think that living a normal life wouldn't be a possibility?

Sophia came forward to fetch her brothers from the altar of Liam. "Back inside now, you two. Let Mr. Liam and his guest stay in peace."

He nodded at the boys as they scampered off. But then he noticed that Sophia was staying put, slipping that onion into an apron pocket, then sliding a glance to Jenny as if to ask why she was with Liam.

Great. How should he frame the introductions?

Jenny, this is Sophia, who's too sweet for the likes of me, even though she and her parents drop bomblike hints about how they'd love for me to ask her out. Sophia, this is Jenny, and really, I have no idea how to explain her to you....

Sophia ended up cutting through the silence. "Would you like to eat now, Liam?"

"I'm not quite up for a meal yet," he said. "I'm meeting the crew at the park in an hour for a round of hoops."

Her expression fell until Jenny spoke up.

"Aw, maybe just a drink?" she asked, mischief in her tone. "What do you say?"

Sophia was all over that, knowing his usual bar order: beer in a bottle. She asked Jenny what she wanted, too.

"Just a diet cola," Jenny answered.

"Coming right up." Sophia flashed Liam a wide smile and was off.

Liam wandered into the nest of café tables, then pulled out a chair for Jenny. "Suddenly you're thirsty."

"I have time for a drink." She sat down, thanking him after he pushed her chair in. Then he took a seat, too.

"I had to do it," Jenny said, unfolding a linen napkin to put on her lap.

"Do what?" he asked. "Ask me out on a date?"

He was teasing, but he wanted to hear her answer, to see her bare reaction, even though he knew it could only be one that would disappoint him.

She fiddled with the place setting, robbing him of the ability to read her. "Sophia was dying for you to sit down. Who am I to rob her of your company?"

"Troublemaker."

Maybe some weird time-space continuum thing would happen right now and it'd swallow him into the cracks of another dimension. Anything to save him from Jenny's screwing around with his personal life.

"Really," she said, "I mean it. Haven't you ever noticed that she's got a crush on you?"

Okay, now, how did a guy tell a girl that she was one of the biggest complications to getting together with a nice woman like Sophia? Besides the fact that Sophia also deserved so much more than he could offer, of course.

A clueless Jenny wasn't finished; she actually seemed to think that she was helping him to get over some kind of shyness with the waitress.

"She's obviously wondering why I'm here with you," Jenny said. "You should just tell her that we're…"

She searched for a description with a wave of her hand.

"We're what?" he asked, his voice ragged.

Damn it, he shouldn't have ventured the question, but it was too late now.

And, in a way, he was glad he'd asked.

Her gaze was hard to read. "I'd say we've become friends. Wouldn't you?"

His heart dipped a little at that.

Friends?

Hell, truthfully, it was all he could handle, and he knew it.

"Friends is good," he said.

He could've sworn that her smile became too forced before she smoothed the napkin in her lap. "So, friend. Where would you take Sophia on your first date?"

"Nowhere."

"What's that? I thought I just heard you say 'nowhere.'"

"Listen, Jenny, I'm sure you've been privy to the rumors. I'm not great boyfriend material."

Funny, he'd spent a long time hoping she would never catch on to that. But now that she'd defined what they were to each other, some of the pressure was off to impress her.

Even so, deep down, there was still a flicker. A ridiculous hope…

Jenny was tilting her head, considering him. "I'll admit that the Club sometimes talks about how you're a man-about-town. But with the whole dude-of-mystery thing you've cultivated, I didn't know if it was true."

The fact that she'd wondered about his personal life sent a bolt of excitement through him. "There're just some guys who aren't built for relationships. I'm upfront about that."

"All right." She adjusted her place mat. "At least you're honest. I've known some men who haven't been quite as forthcoming, and those are the ones who cause the most trouble for a girl."

At his puzzled glance, she added, "They pretend they're there for the long term, and once they get a woman in bed, they're suddenly not available anymore."

Liam blinked at her honesty.

"It's true," she said. "Not that I made that mistake. I mean, I dated a lot, but I was picky. Real picky."

What did she mean by that? Jenny had dated frequently, and it'd burned him to think that she was loving other men. But was she saying she hadn't…? That she didn't…?

"So what you're telling me," she added, fixing a frank gaze on him, "is that you're better behaved than what I encountered?"

As he searched for an answer—he would never call himself well-behaved—Sophia came out with their drinks.

Thank God.

But Liam couldn't help noticing that the young woman had taken her curly brown hair out of its bun and allowed it to fly free. Jenny noticed, too. He knew it because she was making a real effort to drink her cola and not stare at their waitress, who seemed ready to stay and chat for a while.

But when the sound of rising giggles and a crash came from the restaurant, she zoomed off with a frustrated groan.

"Mom and Pop are away for the moment," she said to Liam over her shoulder, "and I have watch-the-monsters duty. I'll be right back out here to take orders for appetizers if you want."

"Not today," Liam said. "Put this on my tab, though?"

Already through the door, Sophia nodded.

Liam had been thankful for the distraction of her, because he'd said enough about his private life to Jenny already. Actually, he wasn't sure how much more there was to say without opening himself with the foolishness of a man who had no reason to share with such an out-of-bounds woman.

He turned the conversation toward her now. "So fair is fair between friends. Why aren't you rushing home to go out on one of those dates? You used to have every Wednesday night booked, as I recall."

Too late, he thought that maybe he shouldn't have said that last part. Damn it, he knew that her medical issue had no doubt put the kibosh on active dating for the time being. She'd even been talking about dating in the past tense a few minutes ago.

"I'm…" She pensively stirred her drink with her straw, but it didn't seem as if he had dampened her willingness to talk. "I'm just taking a break. Besides, I think I've dated every single guy around who matches my wants and needs."

"All right, I've got to ask—"

"What's on that list?"

He settled back in his chair, indeed very curious.

She held up her hands. "Your basic type who's supposed to be found by the hundreds in a place like San Francisco. Ambitious, nicely put together. A guy who enjoys the theater as well as a Judd Apatow comedy. One who's not intimidated by how far I want to get in my career."

"Not such a tough list."

"I don't think so. But it seems we're both wrong."

He wanted to tell her that maybe she hadn't been looking in the right places, that maybe if she just adjusted a requirement or two—if she maybe knocked off the theater and the "nicely put together" parts—she might have an easier time.

Especially if she looked right in front of her.

"Have you ever found anyone who comes close to your ideal?" he asked.

"A couple of times." She gave him a should-I-really-tell-you look.

Maybe it was the fall afternoon, with the crimsoned leaves scuttling along the streets and the air carrying a trace of crispness. Or maybe she saw her life turning like those leaves and it inspired her to go along with the changes. Either way, she continued.

"I found one of those men way back in college," she said as she went back to stirring her drink. "The other was more recent. Franklin. We dated for a few years before we realized things were going nowhere at all."

Liam crossed his arms over his chest. A few years was a long time, and he hadn't expected serial-dater Jenny to have taken part in something so lengthy. The revelation put even more distance between what he was and what she no doubt wanted.

"We had an amiable breakup a while ago," she went on. "We'd talked about marriage every so often, but in the end, we both had to admit that it just wasn't happening for us if we could never decide that committing forever was what we truly wanted. There was always a business trip for one of us that put off our plans, or a vacation we wanted to take, or…something."

He could tell by the thickness of her voice that she wished she could find a person she could be sure about—one who perhaps even struck her affections so hard that she would have no doubts whatsoever that she wanted to be with him. But he also wondered if she was asking herself if there was any man who would take her if that lump turned out to be more.

Liam's next thought rattled him: he would take her, if he were in any shape to.

Grabbing his beer, he prepared to take a sip.

"I can't say I miss Franklin himself as much as…" She sighed. "Being with him."

His bottle hadn't even reached his lips. "Are you talking about…?"

"Sex?"

She laughed, probably because he looked so flummoxed at her having mentioned it.

"McCree," she said, "please don't tell me you think I've been sleeping with every man I date."

"I didn't…" He trailed off, because he'd been about to say that he didn't think about her dating habits at all. But he had to strike that. "I wasn't sure."

"I don't make public announcements, but I don't mind clarifying it, either. Sex isn't something to flip around, you know?"

Jenny. Sex.

His stomach felt as light as the bubbled beer in the bottle that he still held halfway to his mouth.

"Am I taking this new 'friend' thing between us too far?" she asked. "You look weirded out."

"I'm not at all." He finally took a swig.

"It's just…" She leaned her elbows on the table. "I can be a pretty blunt person, and because I'm one of the only women in my office, I'm comfortable around guys in general. Sometimes even more than I am with women, actually, unless you count the Sudsers—but they're more like family."

"Really, I'm fine with the blunt talk." It was just that talking about sex with Jenny was…

Well, too much.

It lit his libido on fire, made the blood crash to places better left calm while he was with her. But he could see just how much he'd freed her up around him with his revelation about the accident, and he wasn't about to lose what he'd already won with her.

He grinned, encouraging her to keep talking, yet

when she did continue, he almost wished he'd put a stop to it when he had the chance.

"I probably shouldn't talk about sex anyway," she said. "To anyone."

He felt the change in tone, the return of the sad Jenny from last week, and he sat up in his chair, willing to fight for the other Jenny to stay.

"Don't tell me you're getting shy on the subject," he said.

"No, that's not it at all." Her gaze clouded. "I'm just not in a place where I should be dwelling on it. Right now, boyfriends seem like such a distant notion, and don't ask why, because…" She grabbed her drink. "Well, just do me a favor and don't, okay?"

He didn't—he just took her comment as a warning to be thankful that she'd decided to be friends with him.

And that he would never be anything more.

Sophia returned to the table, but as far as Liam was concerned, she was welcome.

Because any chance he'd hoped for with Jenny had passed, along with the ticking countdown of their afternoon together.

After their drinks, Jenny had felt the need to escape reality again, even though she'd done just that for much of the afternoon with Liam. But returning to her apartment to finish her work for the day seemed like a much easier way to forget, and she worked on the Thayer presentation until she really couldn't do much more without getting together with the rest of her team tomorrow.

The minute she stacked her paperwork in neat piles

on her home office desk, a heaviness consumed her as the biopsy nudged into her mind again. The only time it'd really left her was when she was around her friends. Especially when she was around Liam, who was becoming more and more important to her by the day.

But why dwell on something she had no intention of pursuing? In her present state, she would only end up making a horror show of anything that might happen between the two of them anyway, and that wasn't fair to him at all. Let someone like that waitress, Sophia, have a crack at him instead, she thought, recalling how the girl had gazed at Liam.

Yet even as the memory settled, a pang of jealousy stabbed at Jenny.

She told herself that the sensation wasn't due as much to how Sophia had looked at Liam as to how Jenny wished she could be the other woman—attractive, feminine, not afraid of what tomorrow might bring. Liam had denied any interest, of course, yet Jenny couldn't understand how he could resist someone so gorgeous and available in favor of sitting at that table with her.

Maybe that was what friends did, she thought, trying to make sense of it all. They enjoyed their time together to the exclusion of anyone else who might be around.

And she'd made the right choice in choosing him as a friend and a friend only.

Feeling better now, she decided to get out of the apartment before evening came around, to make the most of daylight before they had to set their clocks back an hour in less than a couple of weeks. So she grabbed a pair of vintage roller skates that she'd bought in a fit of nostalgic delight one day and then walked ten minutes to the park, where the even pavement would provide a place to glide around.

Not that exercising now would change any results next Wednesday—God, her appointment was coming up so soon—but she was damned if she'd sit around feeling sorry for herself.

After she strapped her skates onto her shoes, she tested them out, wobbly at first, but gaining her balance soon enough. She'd done a lot of skating around in her driveway as a kid, and she felt as carefree and light as she had back then, when the most pressing worry had been getting her homework done for the night.

She sailed along the grass-lined paths, past signs advertising Halloween events in the park, past people walking their dogs and saying "good afternoon" to her. Soon, she found herself beyond the gazebo-strewn picnic areas and at the sports facilities, where a playground preceded tennis and basketball courts.

There was a game on one of them—six men dribbling a ball and dodging each other as they took shots at the backboards.

And Liam was one of the players.

She'd come here not just to skate, but also because, back at Amati's, she'd heard him mention a game, and catching a glimpse of him in his element had caught her fancy.

And maybe she wanted to find out if the lone wolf really did have other friends.

She skated toward the game, slowing to a stop far enough away that Liam wouldn't see her yet. His leg didn't seem to hold him back from stealing the ball from a man wearing blue sweats with a Rolling Stones logo on the front, then executing a perfect shot from beyond the three-point line. As she watched him move, her body went warm with appreciation.

Liam looked more like an athlete and less like a Laundromat ne'er-do-well now, with his dark sweats and a gray T-shirt damp with perspiration. His longish hair was pushed back from a face intense with the thrill of competition, and with a carnal flash, she imagined touching his slick skin, feeling it against her own.

She started to throb at the unexpected fantasy—at the imagined passion on his face, in his every move.

If she kissed him, she'd feel the burn of his face against her softer cheeks. If he caressed her, she'd revel in feeling a man appreciating her body before it might undergo a change that would alter her life in so many ways, maybe even making her hide under these baggy clothes for a long time to come.

But Liam…he'd undergone a physical change himself. Would he be one of the few who could understand what she was going through?

In her fantasies, she saw that he did, and she allowed herself one more moment of stimulation, of feeling someone else against her, body to body….

Then she realized that she was standing here, watching him, while desire marked her like a beacon in the middle of the park. So before he saw her, she began to wheel around, to leave, because she didn't want him to think she'd been following him like a crazed puppy or something.

Even though that was pretty much exactly what she'd been doing.

Then she heard the players raising their voices to each other, heard Liam above all the rest of them.

"Jenny?" he called.

Her stomach somersaulted, celebrating that he'd caught her before she'd skated away.

But, darn it, he'd caught her before she'd skated away.

Was he wondering what the heck she was doing here when she'd told him earlier that she wasn't interested in dating anyone?

Taking a stabilizing breath, she faced him, waved, then glided over to where he was standing behind the chain-link fence, grinning as if he'd known all along that she would show up.

And when she got close enough to see the sparkle of his eyes, she swallowed, because she'd known it, too.

"Couldn't stay away, could you?" he asked playfully.

But she recognized an even deeper question in his gaze.

Why did *you come?*

Or maybe that was only the echo of a question she couldn't even answer herself.

Chapter Six

Liam's heart pounded at the sight of Jenny on the other side of the fence.

She was wearing skates and a pair of jeans covered by one of those baggy tops and jackets, but in spite of her dressing down, she looked so fresh, so flushed, that he couldn't help holding on to the chain-link just to keep himself from climbing over the barrier and taking her in his arms.

He still couldn't believe she was standing here. Hell, when he'd first caught sight of her, he'd had to look twice.

Yet when he'd realized that his eyes weren't playing tricks on him, he'd given up the basketball he'd been about to shoot, then moved to the fence to call to her, out of breath, out of his mind.

Now, in back of him, the guys bounced the ball and shuffled around.

"Get back in the game, McCree!"

"This ain't halftime!"

But Liam only held up his hand to clam them up. They realized that sometimes, he had to duck out when his leg needed rest, and for all they knew, this was one of those times.

Then again, they no doubt saw the pretty girl on the other side of the fence.

He turned back to Jenny, and she gestured to his crowd.

"Maybe you'd better oblige your pals by scooting back in there?" she said.

"Nah. They've already been trounced enough, and they don't know when to admit they've taken a licking." He pushed a hank of damp hair back from his forehead. "Unless you came around here with the intention of joining the game..."

"You wouldn't be able to keep up."

She sounded like the gave-as-good-as-she-got Jenny of old, but with those roller skates on, he had to chuckle at her bravado.

Catching on to the source of his amusement, she pushed off and whirled in a dainty circle, then ended on a tah-dah pose.

"All I'm missing is a headband and disco music, right?" she asked.

"I just never would've guessed you had this in you."

"Likewise." She nodded to the guys, who'd officially ended the game and were now packing it up and calling it a day. "I wasn't even sure that you had buddies outside the Laundromat, yet here you are, dribbling a basketball around with a few of them."

Whoa. She'd thought he didn't have friends?

And to think, he'd only been trying to play it cool in the Club.

"I came off as a real loner, did I?" he asked.

"You just seemed like one of those people who functions pretty well on his own. That's all."

Damn, that sounded sad.

He glanced at the guys, who noisily made their way across the court, dressed in their sweat jackets and tossing the ball back and forth.

"Actually," he said, "since I moved to Placid Valley, I've met quite a few new people. But it can take time to fall in with the ones you're most compatible with. I didn't run into this bunch until a few months ago. One of them owns a music shop on Orange Blossom Road. The rest like to hang out there. They all invited me to round out their games."

As if summoned, a couple of the men came to razz Liam while rounding to the other side of the fence and saying goodbye. Liam good-naturedly promised to be at another game in a few days. Meanwhile, he could see them checking out Jenny, wondering who she was and why she'd had the power to stop him midshoot.

Liam quickly introduced her with the title of "friend" they'd settled on that afternoon, but he noticed how his teammates smirked at each other.

"Hey, don't you all have lives to lead?" he asked, hoping to get them on their way.

Carl, the music shop owner, dribbled the ball once,

then tucked it under his arm. "We were kind of thinking we'd hang around."

A seventies music fanatic named Jack stole the ball from his pal. "Jenny, what kind of shot are you?"

She was about to answer, but Liam gave them the evil eye and said, "See you in a couple of days," making it clear that it really was time for them to scram.

The two men laughed, said goodbye to Jenny, then walked off, making "okay" signs behind her.

Thank God she didn't turn around and see.

"Sorry to have broken things up," Jenny said.

"They need to get home to their families, anyway." He backed away from the fence. "Wait here while I get my stuff?"

She tugged her jacket tighter around her, as if only now realizing that by showing up and ending the game, she'd gotten stuck with him.

But why would he even think that, when there was the hint of a smile on her mouth and, more important, in her eyes?

His heart kicked at his chest as he jogged to the other side of the court for his sweat jacket. Then, taking great care to pretend that there wasn't a twinge of pain in his leg, he fought a slight limp on the way back while yanking on his jacket and exiting the court.

He joined her on the pavement outside, running his fingers through his disheveled hair and wishing he resembled one of those put-together men Jenny had told him she'd earmarked for relationship material. Chances were that sweats hadn't been high on her wants list.

But she didn't seem to mind how he looked as she

rolled along next to him. With the skates on, she was taller than usual, coming up to his nose, and the clover scent of her hair teased him just as it had earlier today.

God help him.

He spied a lemonade stand near the edge of the playground and headed toward it, as he always did after a game. A neon-markered sign taped to a large orange cooler on the table read LEMONADE $1.00 HOT CHOCOLATE $1.25.

"Entrepreneurs," he told Jenny while the three young girls in ponytails and braids poured drinks for the elderly couple ahead in line. One of the kids' moms sat on a bench nearby, supervising while chatting with another woman.

"Location, location, location," Jenny said. "Smart to have beverages for the thirsty players who come off the courts."

She reached into her jacket for her chic wallet.

"Hold up," Liam said, raising his own billfold out of habit. "It's on me."

"But you paid for happy hour."

"What can I say? My expense account is huge."

He extracted the bills, then ordered from the girls.

Jenny came to hover next to him, her arm almost brushing his and making the hair on his skin stand at attention.

"All right," she said, "I'm not going to argue. There's something to be said for grateful acceptance, so thank you."

He almost told her that the biggest repayment she could give him was to treat him like a friend, to maybe even start calling him by his first name.

But hadn't even that changed lately?

Hadn't his last name taken on a sort of affectionate softness, like she'd seen something wedged between the "Mc" and the "Cree" that not many others had ever discovered?

He delivered a hot chocolate to Jenny's waiting hands, and she wrapped her fingers around the foam cup, then blew on the surface to part the steam.

He couldn't help watching her lips.

God, they were full and so naturally red, even a little pouty, like Marilyn Monroe's had been. He imagined they'd be soft under his own, and the mere thought tangled his body into a fused mass of electricity.

They left the stand, Jenny slowly skating along by his side while she carefully saw to it that her drink didn't spill.

"When I was as old as those girls," she said, "I had my own business, too."

"Let me guess. You were already marketing your parents' walnuts."

She gave him a wide-eyed glance. "Am I that transparent?"

He was pleased that he'd been on target. "I can put two and two together. They had a crop and you had the ambition, even back in the fourth grade, I imagine. But how exactly did you plan to dominate the walnut world?"

"I organized our own roadside stand and thought of ways to persuade the kids at school to buy packages for their brownies at home. Then I'd research different recipes that contained walnuts, share them with my friends and just oh-so-conveniently have a package or two with me so they could bring them home to mommy or daddy." She laughed. "The administration had to put a stop to it, but I made a few bucks nonetheless."

She smiled at him, as if she still couldn't believe he'd guessed so easily.

But he'd gotten to know Jenny through listening, through paying the kind of attention a man should pay a woman when he valued every word she uttered.

"I hope," he said, "that your boss appreciates the hell out of you."

Her skate wheels hit a crack in the pavement, and she almost spilled her cocoa.

He reached out to steady her, his hand going to the small of her back. For an eternal moment, he reveled in the curve of it, wishing he could leave his hand in the soft, provocative place. But, knowing better, he backed away while she kept watching him, her face flushed. Then, after tucking a stray hair behind her ear, she began rolling along again.

He took big gulps of his lemonade.

"Not likely," she said. "In fact—and I can't believe I'm saying this—work isn't as hospitable as it used to be."

Her voice was flat now, and he cursed under his breath at choosing the wrong subject. Yet when she continued, he realized that maybe she needed to talk about it. That maybe through the dumb luck of his Irish, Liam was here at the right time for her again. And when she went on to tell him about her uncleared absences at Kendrick Corporation and about the official discussion her boss had initiated about rules the other day, he was only too happy to have been available.

"Let me get this straight," he said when she'd finished. "Your company would sacrifice a creative, hard worker like you just because of some rules that don't really reflect your effort?"

But he wanted to ask her something more. *Haven't you told him* why *you've been absent?*

"Findley doesn't really have a choice about those rules," Jenny said. "The corporation makes them and he's there to enforce them."

"And that right there is exactly why I'm not a corporate guy." Liam crumpled his emptied cup in one hand and tossed it into a trash can. "Jenny, have you ever thought about leaving that place? Because, excuse me if I'm wrong, but it makes no sense to labor under an iron fist."

She rolled to a stop, her skates rumbling, her hands still cupped around her hot chocolate, as if she needed something to hold on to.

"That job is really all I have," she said softly. "It's all that's keeping me sane."

He'd stopped, too, because she'd just answered his private question about why she hadn't told the boss the reason for her absences.

But what platitudes could he offer now?

I understand why you might be clinging to something that's always made you come off like a superstar, Jenny. You need to focus on whatever is good in your life so you can beat back those worries about your health.

But he wasn't sure what to tell her without bringing up the subject and letting her know that *he* knew. Besides, she'd made it clear earlier that she didn't want him to ask what was wrong, even though that didn't stop her from hinting about it.

He also didn't want to give her any excuse to leave

him standing here because she was angry or embarrassed that he'd overheard her secret.

Instead, he did all he could do to keep her from falling when she was doing such a hell of a job of standing under circumstances that would bring lesser people to their knees.

"No matter what happens," he said, "you've got to know that you're valuable, Jenny. Your company isn't the ultimate authority on what you're made of, because they have no damned idea."

Her breath was shaky as she exhaled. "I'll admit, the consequences of getting fired have crossed my mind. If it happened, I have a lot of money saved up. The paychecks have always been nice, so it's not like I'm financially destitute if the worst happened. And I'd still be eligible for COBRA benefits—"

She cut herself off, and he knew it was because she thought she shouldn't be talking about insurance and health to him.

He grinned at her, trying so hard to cheer her. "It sounds like I don't even need to offer you a job in my company again."

"Well, you *could* offer."

She smiled a little, and he ached that much more.

He walked closer to her. "I'd give you a million opportunities to team up with me, even if you turned down every one of them." Then he lowered his voice. "My offer's always open."

She must've sensed that he was referring to so much more than work, too—there was also the chance for her to confide in him if she wanted to.

And, in spite of all his misgivings, there was the offer of his heart.

But he couldn't reveal that, because she'd told him straight out that a boyfriend wasn't in the cards, and he wouldn't put her in a position to have to deal with any unwanted attentions.

It'd be selfish when what she really needed right now was another friend.

"An open offer." She rested the cup against her chest, looking at the ground. "How can you have such confidence in me without knowing me very well at all?"

"I'd bet on you any day of the week. For anything."

At that, she finally glanced at him, the sun shedding light on her as it began its descent. The muted slant of it made her hair all the more golden.

Was she getting that he believed in her in more than just business? That he knew she could beat any kind of adversity?

"Can I be honest?" she asked.

Oh, great. Had he revealed too much?

"Sure," he said, waiting for the hammer to fall.

Yet there was only a slight catch in her voice as she spoke. "I came to this park because I was lonely, and I knew you were playing ball. I hoped I'd find you, but I was afraid you'd think I was here because…"

His pulse sputtered. "Because why?"

She obviously didn't know what to say. Or maybe she just didn't know how to say it.

He wanted her to admit that she was just as attracted to him as he was to her, wanted to get the guessing games out of the way once and for all.

But who was he to think that Liam McCree, of all people, would be enough to sustain her during a hard time?

So he told himself to be grateful for what he had with her and leave it at that.

He started walking again, taking a handful of her jacket to gently pull her along on her skates. "You came here to watch a friend play ball," he said. "You don't have to say anything more, Jenny."

When she linked arms with him, his skin seemed to flare with heat, but the emotional sheen in her eyes touched his heart and overwhelmed every base urge.

"Thank you," she whispered.

He couldn't say a word, because her acceptance was enough to drill him.

Perforating all those damned shields he'd been putting up.

The next day, Jenny reported for work fully energized and spurred by last night's pep talk from Liam.

She *was* good at what she did. She *was* valuable.

And she should have never forgotten that.

Hence, she spent the day developing the Thayer presentation with her partner Bryan, who kept giving her high fives every time she came up with a great idea.

Nothing could bring her down.

Even though, in the back of her mind, she kept feeling a niggle, a growing question of whether she'd been placing too much emphasis on work.

But there was no time to think of that while the team members were in their own offices, taking care of their individual portions of the project. Hers included designing the PowerPoint show, and she was brainstorming and sketching ideas for graphics.

Her cell phone rang, and she saw her mother's number on the call screen, then answered, intending to chat and work at the same time since Findley was atending an out-of-office meeting. She was being effective anyway, though, especially because she'd been putting in so many hours at home.

"Hey, Mom," she said, picturing her mother, with her fading blond hair and big blue eyes under a pair of tortoiseshell glasses, pacing with the phone to her ear.

"Jenny, sweetie, I only meant to leave a message. I know you must be busy."

"Never too busy for you and Dad." She sketched a concept for a modern, efficient butler—one that would reflect the classiness as well as the user-friendliness of their product. "How's everything?"

"That's what I called to ask you."

"Mom, you worry too much. I'm feeling fine."

"It's only that you take so much on yourself, and your father and I get concerned that you don't have anyone around to help. What if we flew out there for a while? What would you think of that?"

"As I told you last week, I'd think it's unnecessary to have you traipse here from Florida." Glancing around, Jenny checked to see that no one would overhear her. "If I get any more bad news, then it'd be appropriate for you to spend all that money to come out here. Otherwise, please, Mom, let's not make something out of what might only be a scare."

How was it that she was the calm one now instead of the other way around? Maybe there was just something about having to soothe someone else that distanced her from what was really happening.

"You said you have people helping you?" her mom asked.

"Yes, Mei's been absolutely great."

"How about a support group? Jenny, I've been doing online research, and there are a lot of options out there."

"I know—you've been sending me links in your e-mails." Jenny stopped sketching. "But I've got other friends."

And she'd found herself seeking out one of them last night, then talking to him as if he already knew about her lump. It'd only seemed to be a natural extension of their previous conversations and, much to her surprise, she'd found Liam easier to confide in than she'd ever expected.

Maybe that was because she suspected he'd over-heard her confessing to Mei about the lump, though. That actually helped, since she could talk to him without *really* talking to him. With Liam, she could bounce ideas off him without expecting the discomfort of pity.

Her mom clucked her tongue. "Jenny, you're too in-dependent for your own good."

"I really do have support." A stinging heat crept into her throat as she thought of Liam again. "More than I ever expected."

Suddenly she became aware of a presence just outside the window next to her closed door and, seeing Findley outside, she hustled to sign off, telling her mom she would call her later tonight. Then she tucked her phone into the pocket of her no-nonsense black business jacket as her boss knocked on her door.

Jenny told him to come in, and he strolled into her office. Smiling at him, she continued sketching.

"Jennifer."

His tone sounded defeated, and she stopped sketching when she noticed that his hair wasn't quite as neat as usual, that his tie was slightly crooked.

He closed her door behind him to a crack, then sat in a chair that faced her.

"Pete," she said, her stomach in knots. Pete Findley didn't do casual office chatting, but here he was.

"I was at a corporate meeting, and…" Running his hand through his hair, he sighed. "I'm just going to come out with it. The news isn't good."

Her mind went into a numb limbo, where she heard everything he was saying, but it took a moment to understand his meaning.

He continued. "I knew this was coming, but I was hoping they'd change their minds. That didn't quite happen today."

"Change their minds about what?"

She sounded so calm. How?

Maybe it was because, in the back of her head, she heard Liam telling her that she was worth more than what she was getting from this job.

"Lay-off." Findley met Jenny's gaze straight on.

Fired? she thought, the word jumbled into random letters, then finally coming together in a *pow!* of realization.

She was getting fired, except that it wasn't for being written up three times.

With all the work, the planning, the effort she'd put into impressing the compny, it hadn't even mattered.

Everything—the pressure here at work, the pressure she'd put on herself to do well, the loss of control when it came to the health of her body—all crashed in on her at once, and she slowly rose from her chair.

"Have I really done such a terrible job?"

"Jennifer, I know you've had a rough patch lately, but this is strictly based on seniority, not by choice. I was hoping they'd let us branch bosses have some input…."

"Am I *ever* going to be good enough?"

The question ricocheted inside her, chipping away until it revealed an epiphany.

She'd tried so, so hard to deny it, but even a job couldn't replace what had deserted her when she'd heard about the lump. The shock had robbed her of confidence, and she *hadn't* gotten that back here at work, had she?

His expression regretful, Findley leaned over and shut the door the rest of the way, and Jenny felt the last of what she'd been clinging to slip out of her grasp.

She grabbed at the desk to hold on to something.

Anything.

Afterward, Jenny had packed up her desk and gone down to the parking garage to sit in her Lexus, where she was currently gripping the steering wheel.

Trying to find something else to hold on to.

She wasn't "one of the boys" anymore. She wasn't the company hotshot.

So who *was* she?

She'd called Mei already, her tone anesthetized, and her friend had done her best to soothe her. But Mei and Travis had important plans for tonight, and she was running around with her hair on fire while prepping a small party where they would announce her pregnancy to their parents.

Jenny could handle this without Mei, right? And she could even deal with this latest twist in her life without worrying her parents, either.

She'd tell them when she'd gotten herself under better control.

So she drove home, barely seeing the stoplights and the roads stretching out before her. And before she knew it, she was cruising down the avenue toward her apartment, past the Suds Club, where a light shone from the Laundromat in the dusk.

Always open, she thought.

As she slowed down, she saw that the room was empty except for someone doing wash by the machines at the front window.

Liam?

Her hands had started to tremble, so she pulled over to the curb and cut the engine, admitting to herself that she didn't want to go home, to be alone.

How pathetic was that?

Her, Ms. Strong and Independent Single Girl, U.S.A.

But was there any shame in needing to tell someone how crummy her day had been? Especially Liam, who would comfort her with righteous anger about how corporations sucked anyway.

It was just what she needed to hear, pathetic or not.

She got out of the car, locked it, then crossed the sidewalk to enter the Laundromat.

The bell sounded on the door, catching Liam's attention as he stood away from the grumbling washing machine.

At first he smiled, but the expression faded into one of deep concern.

"Jenny?" he asked.

"I…"

She'd been holding in her mortification at being rejected for so long that it burst out of her with a sob.

"What happened?" he said, coming over to her.

Before she covered her face, she saw that he was reaching out to her, as if unsure of what to do.

"It's okay," she managed to say, trying to be brave, even though she was quite aware that she'd become an instant disaster. "I'm just… It's stress. One big blast of stress."

He touched her arm, and her chest constricted, then pushed out a few more words.

"It's my job," she said, wiping her face now, even while a few more tears trickled out.

"What about your job?"

He sounded ticked, as if ready to come to her aid if she needed it. Her heart swelled.

"Laid off." She performed a shrug that was meant to be fatalistically casual, but she lost her composure when another sob escaped.

Nowhere to go…

"Unbelievable." He sounded floored. Then his voice turned gruff. "Those idiots."

"I know, huh?" She hitched in a breath, huffed it out and fought the tears again.

"You'll be back at a better place under better circumstances in no time. Believe me."

"Right." She sniffed. "I know you're right."

She wiped at her face again, took another deep breath and looked up at him.

His eyes had a glow to them—anger for her sake, concern.

And something else that sent a shock wave through her.

"You're always going to land on your feet," he said, softer now, his voice hoarse as he came closer, inches away.

She nodded, so inexplicably drawn to him.

Would it be wrong to take a step nearer? He smelled so good. Felt so good this close to her.

She took that step, and suddenly they were a breath apart.

"Jenny," he whispered, reaching out to touch her hair, then her cheek.

She closed her eyes under the rushing comfort, the knowledge that she could lean against him if she needed to.

And she did need, but it wasn't because of the job.

She knew that as clear as day.

Canting into his touch, she placed her palm over his hand, feeling the roughness of his skin. A male's skin, an intimate contact that swirled desire through her as if she were being stirred into an entirely different woman.

Emboldened, she stopped listening to the what-ifs and just gave in to what her body wanted, standing on her tiptoes and pressing her mouth against his.

Chapter Seven

Every fantasy Liam had ever harbored about Jenny exploded the second her lips touched his.

Her kiss was a free fall from a mountaintop with the ground rushing up at him and blasting against him with a full-body slam.

It was…everything.

Forgetting all the caution he'd imposed upon himself with Jenny, he kissed her back, slipping his hands underneath her jaws, as if he were cupping her and drinking her in. His palms tingled with the feel of her smooth skin, with the reality of actually touching her.

As she nestled closer, pressing her mouth against his slowly, tentatively, his thoughts blanked out altogether except for the feel of those lips on his.

Those lush, cherry lips.

They were just as head-spinningly delicious as he'd always known they'd be. So soft while he sipped at her. So carnal yet innocent as he pressed harder against her mouth with a growing passion that insisted he take this farther, deeper.

But even as his libido drove him on, his heart told him to ease it down.

So he came up for a breath and rubbed his mouth against hers, then gave her smaller kisses on the tips of her lips while tracing his fingers down her neck, then up. He was memorizing every inch of flesh in case this dream came to a crashing end.

"Jenny," he whispered against her, as if he was making sure she was really here.

He skimmed her cheekbone with his fingertips, and she sighed under his mouth, bringing the kiss to a languorous pause with their lips still poised over each other's, their foreheads touching.

Her breathing was soft yet strained, as if she were sorting through her muddled senses, and he paced his own intake of air, too, unsure of what was going to happen next.

"Wow," she said on a whisper.

Wow. That was a good sign, wasn't it? It showed that she'd been just as affected as he had.

Or had she said it because she was surprised she'd initiated such intimacy between them?

He sketched his fingers over her throat and rested his thumb at the dip between her collarbones.

Hot, he thought. Her skin was burning.

Yet the heat could've also been from his own frayed nerve endings.

As he circled his thumb into that sensual cove at the base of her neck, he started to become even more aroused, the blood churning through him to dangerous areas. Should he say something to keep this moment from breaking?

His voice was close to a murmur. "The last thing I expected tonight was to find us in this position."

At the play of his fingers, her breathing had quickened again. "This isn't what I had in mind when I came in here, Liam. It's as much of a surprise to me as it is to you."

The sound of his name on her lips almost took him out at the knees.

She swallowed, and he felt her throat work. Felt her pulse bumping against his palm in erratic time.

Then she shifted, moving back an inch so that their foreheads weren't touching anymore. She was taking in air with longer, deeper efforts, and that excited him to an even wilder extent.

But she had also stiffened, and that sent an alert through him.

He coaxed his hand from her neck to her shoulder, a position that seemed so much safer in this tense aftermath.

Just take it slowly, he thought, feeling as if the world had sped to a million miles an hour within the past few minutes.

As she searched his gaze, he tried his best not to put up those shields that he used with everyone else. When he'd seen Jenny walk in here looking so devastated, he'd all but fallen apart himself, not knowing specifically what had gone wrong while still realizing that he wanted to right whatever was plaguing her.

"I suppose," she finally said, a small smile curving her mouth, "that I've been curious about what it'd be like to kiss you. And it…just happened."

He couldn't help watching her lips, reliving the way they'd fit against his so perfectly. "I'm glad it just happened. I've been waiting for it, too, Jenny. For a real long time."

The confession rolled out between them like a cloud changing shape and form, trying to decide what it was going to be.

Through the haze of it, he saw that her eyes had brightened, and the light from her reaction lanced his chest. But then she seemed to remember everything else outside the protected bubble of these past few moments, and her gaze darkened.

He didn't know what to do to keep her fleeting happiness from disappearing altogether. Damn it, they'd just gotten somewhere, and now they'd have to take a step back?

Not if he could help it.

He kept his hand on her shoulder, as if that would make all the difference. But their moment—the fast-forward motion, the hard-to-breathe, pulse-pummeling interlude—seemed to have already elapsed.

It was all there in her eyes, even though her voice hadn't changed a bit.

"To be honest," she said, "I've been attracted to you for a while, too. But I told myself that you were just a passing fancy because you were so wrong for me. So I kidded around with you, avoiding anything beyond teasing. Yet there was just something…"

"That couldn't be ignored," he finished for her. He ran his thumb over her collarbone, felt her shiver. Their attraction *still* couldn't be ignored.

She took a steadying breath, then reached up to grab his hand from the more intimate spot on her shoulder. But she folded her fingers through his—an affectionate sign.

A friendly one.

His hopes sank. He had a bad feeling about this: now that she wasn't as emotionally off balance, she had gone back to asking him to be a friend, although his own platonic outlook had just shattered with their kiss. She'd reeled him too far in, even beyond the fear that had always kept him uninvolved. And now that he realized it, his pulse escalated.

Should he put his heart in jeopardy? Should he chance everything for more than kisses?

"Jenny," he said, testing, making sure to get his meaning across without revealing that he knew her secret. "Having someone around who cares as much as I do wouldn't make whatever you're going through tougher, if that's what you're thinking."

It was out there now, and he'd never felt more vulnerable.

When she held his hand in both of hers, he knew he should've just kept his mouth shut, his emotions closed.

"I wish that were true," she said wistfully.

Crash.

There was his heart, in pieces on the floor.

He understood her rationale, because in the coming weeks, she'd be going through hell. Even so, in her gentle words, he saw a replay of that night he'd revealed his scars to his girlfriend.

Rejection.

He couldn't stop his defenses from rallying, from saving his pride before it could be fully decimated by someone else who wouldn't accept him the way he came.

"Okay, then," he said, glancing at their entwined hands. "I can accept that we kissed in the heat of a trying moment for you, when you were emotionally scattered, and it didn't mean anything beyond that."

"It did mean a lot." But he could see that she was relieved to have him supposedly on the same page. "And I wouldn't blame you for getting angry with me for being so impetuous."

"I'm not angry."

She seemed even more relieved. "Thank goodness."

How could he ever be mad at her?

Still, he wanted to make excuses, to get past this before she realized that he'd wanted so much more.

"We were just curious," he said, "and we gave in. Now we're all the better for getting it out of the way." He gave a covering laugh. "I can never get past the one-month stage of a relationship, anyway."

"And I haven't had a much better track record lately." She studied him, as if measuring what was still between them. "I mean, can you imagine the awkwardness here in the Club if things went any further with us?"

"Yeah, the Sudsers would always be asking how our dates went and offering advice we wouldn't want to hear."

"And they'd always be watching, just like we were their own private soap opera."

"God forbid." He was doing really well here, pretending as if he hadn't been cut down the middle.

She squeezed his hand. "So…we're still good? I didn't totally blow it by being rash?"

He nodded, because there was nothing else to do if he didn't want to make a big deal out of this and end up upsetting her when she didn't need the extra drama. She had enough to concentrate on without him adding to her problems.

"Still friends," he said, giving her a tweak under the chin, then enclosing her in his arms to seal the deal.

But he had ulterior motives, because with her face against his chest, she would never be able to see him closing his eyes as he pulled her close.

And she would never see the disappointment that had to be written all over his face.

The next day, Jenny and Mei met early at the local market so they could have quality time together and talk about the layoff, with Jenny reassuring Mei that she had lots of savings, and a solid severance package with access to insurance.

A morning outing was the best option because Jenny wasn't going to be able to make it to the Club today; she'd arranged to meet her ex-team member Bryan for lunch to hand over the Thayer notes she'd inadvertently taken with her when she'd cleaned out her desk. It turned out that Bryan, who had two years of seniority over her, had left the building last night before she'd been let go, so a midafternoon farewell with him was the best solution.

Of course, this made her a total sucker, but she cared about how he would come off at work, and she didn't want her exit to hurt any of the remaining members of the team, either.

Mei had felt bad about not being there after Jenny's ordeal, but Jenny wasn't going to countenance any remorse from her friend, because last night had been a happy one for Mei, who was celebrating pregnancy news with the husband with whom she'd been reunited.

Besides, Jenny was far less tragedy-struck than she'd ever expected to be after losing the job she'd thought had meant so much to her.

Oddly, she even felt as if she'd shrugged off a load of chains that had been weighing her down without her even realizing it. But leaving the job behind didn't mean everything was fine and dandy—there were still some links attached to her that felt heavier than ever, because there was a haze surrounding her now, one that enclosed her in a fog of confusion that she couldn't seem to find her way out of.

How would she cope from this point on?

Who was she going to see when she looked at the girl in the baggy clothing in the mirror—a failure? A person who couldn't even handle a career, much less a lump?

All she knew was that last night, she hadn't been asking these questions—or thinking about anything else—when she'd been with Liam.

As she and her best friend strolled down the vegetable aisle in the market, they finished chatting about Jenny's work blues and continued on to the happy subject of Mei's pregnancy-announcement gathering.

Meanwhile, Jenny hugged her arms, rubbing away the goose bumps. Soft generic music played over the sound system while Mei plucked a batch of celery from a water-misted display and put it in the grocery cart.

Jenny felt like a balloon that was close to popping with the news about her and Liam's "moment," but she'd kept it to herself all morning, wondering if sharing it might rob the kiss of its intimacy. She was also feeling guilty for putting Liam in such a position, especially after telling him that she'd only been giving in to impulse.

Mei brought Jenny back with her voice.

"My parents were over the moon to hear that we're having child number two." She rested her hand on her still-flat stomach; she wasn't far enough along to be showing yet. "We'll be telling Travis's dad soon, too, since he couldn't make it last night, but that'll take more finesse since he and Travis have been estranged for a while."

"He's taking steps to mend fences?"

"Yes."

"That's great, Mei. But aren't you going to be partied out by that time?" Jenny saw how tired her friend was, but she had to admit that healing her relationship with Travis had reinvested Mei with a lot of color and energy. "You had the get-together yesterday, then there'll be the one tonight, and now you'll be arranging an event with Grandpa Webb in the near future."

"My family's all about having constant gatherings. I'm used to it." Mei wheeled the cart forward. "Besides, Travis had the crazy urge to invite everyone at the Club over for impromptu appetizers and drinks tonight so he can get to know the people I always talk about. It has to do with this whole new lease on life we're embarking on."

"I see," Jenny said while nonchalantly checking over some avocados. "And you're inviting everyone from the Club who can come on short notice?"

"Is that your way of asking if Liam McCree's on the list?"

"I suppose it is."

A gargantuan flush enveloped her, one so powerful that her skin actually prickled with a hint of sweat. But she should be used to being overcome, since it'd been happening about every three minutes since she'd kissed him with such unrestrained passion.

And when he'd kissed her back with equal fervor.

"Oh, my." Mei had stopped the cart and was staring at Jenny. "Look at that blush on you."

"I'm not blushing."

"If that's not a blush, then you're a new, pink species that hasn't been identified yet. What's going on?"

But then Mei guessed before Jenny could say another word.

"You and Liam McCree?" her friend whispered, her eyes wide.

"It was all very innocent, Mei."

Boy, she sounded calm, but inside, her heart was banging around.

"And what constitutes 'innocent'?" Mei asked.

Jenny's lips began to tingle, and she fought the urge to touch them. "A kiss. I kissed him." And she went on to explain how it all came about after the layoff.

Mei still gaped, as if this were surely a sign of the earth's last days.

But then she leaned closer, whispering.

"What was it like?"

Jenny wasn't sure she could put it into words, but she tried. "Waves crashing, then pulling at me and covering me with this soft kind of motion. Then…more waves."

And she felt the caress of them just as if she were being bathed by warm water that sucked at her, covering her with dissolving bubbles and smooth strokes.

"Oh, that's a very nice way of describing it," Mei said.

Then she fluttered a hand in front of her face, as if needing to cool off.

"Mei," Jenny said, "let's not make a huge deal about it. We both know a kiss isn't going anywhere. It was bound to happen between me and Liam someday, and it did. Now we can all move on."

"What do you mean?"

"I mean he's become…"

She was going to say "a friend" again. But it sure felt like she should be describing him as something much more.

Jenny took over the cart, pushing it ahead. "More kissing just isn't in the cards. Let's put it that way."

Mei rested her hand on Jenny's back. "I can see why you're not willing to commit to anything, and even why you needed a toe-curling kiss last night. But have you ever considered that someone like Liam might be a positive in your life?"

"Sure. But dragging him into what I might have to

face is a recipe for failure. I wouldn't expect any man to give up his comfortable life just so he can go through hard times for a girl he just started dating."

"It'd take a good man to do that, wouldn't it?"

They turned a corner, and Jenny paused in pushing the cart. "Yes, Mei, it'd take a real good man. And you don't have to tell me that Liam is one of them."

Her friend rubbed her back, and in that gesture, Jenny read that good men were hard to find, and once you had one in your sights, you'd better keep him.

But she was so busy grasping at so many other things that her hands were too full to reach out to anyone who might help her weather the coming storm.

When Mei had invited Liam to the get-together, he'd been taken off guard. After all, Suds parties usually took place in the Laundromat itself, like the potluck the crowd had held today.

But then Mei had explained that her husband wanted to meet everyone, and Liam had accepted.

Especially after she had mentioned that Jenny would be there, too.

His *friend,* he repeated to himself, thinking that if he said it enough times, he might come around to accepting it.

So that evening, when he walked into Mei's apartment—a vividly colored place with hardwood floors, rock fountains and pictures of Mei's four-year-old daughter, Isabel, displayed on shelves—he tried not to be obvious about seeking Jenny out.

Yet, damn it, from her place in the kitchen, she

flashed on his radar more than the other six Suds Club members who were in the room.

Even so, he played it easy, congratulating the hosts on their good news, then handing off a bottle of Chianti to Mei. He also shook hands with her husband, Travis—a tanned and buffed firefighter/paramedic with short dark hair and a crooked nose that was rumored to have been earned on the job.

"Looks good," Travis said when Mei showed him Liam's wine. "Thanks for bringing it."

"Thought I should bring something," Liam said, "even though our hostess probably won't be having any."

"Not a drop," she said, patting her tummy, where New Baby Webb was nested. "But can we open this for you, Liam?"

He nodded, and both she and Travis left while a few other Sudsers moseyed up to him to say hi.

Evina, who was garbed in a pink traditional East Indian choli dress, looked as polished as she always did, but Vivian, who normally wore bike shorts, was sporting bold lipstick plus a stylish black dress.

In return, they were marveling at the nighttime version of Liam, even though he hadn't done much more than tame his hair, plus put on some ironed khakis and a tucked-in button-down.

"Someone shines up pretty well," Vivian said, tugging on Liam's shirt.

Evina added her own joking two cents. "We weren't sure who you were from the other side of the room."

Luckily, Vivian's husband and Evina's boyfriend came over to rescue Liam, and after he'd met them, his attention drifted over to the kitchen, where Jenny was arranging hors d'oeuvres on a large plate.

The oxygen stole out of him, because she, too, had "shined up."

Not that she'd needed to, but her turquoise dress, which was covered by the requisite baggy white sweater, loaned a brightness to her eyes that he hadn't seen for a while now. She'd also styled her short hair in its movie-star waves and used a soft, pearled lipstick.

That was mostly what Liam saw from his spot by the couch—her mouth.

The lips he'd kissed last night.

As if connecting to his heightened awareness, Jenny lifted her head, her chest rising in an inhaled breath when she saw him.

Had she been thinking about that kiss, too?

Had it been dogging her as it'd dogged him?

She smiled in greeting, still leaving him unsure, then picked up her dish and brought it to the linen-draped dining table to join the dim sum selections.

By that time, Mei had gone to uncork his wine, and Travis had joined her in the kitchen, touching her face, then her belly. The two smiled lovingly at each other, and Liam glanced away.

But then he realized that the whole room was composed of couples, and that he and Jenny were the only singles around.

How comfortable.

He wandered over to her, taking care to disguise a slight ache in his leg that seemed to be getting worse by the hour. Meanwhile, she grabbed a glass of what looked to be ginger ale from the counter.

"You look festive," he said when he got there, understating his opinion. He didn't want to scare her off by telling her how she'd made his night.

He also didn't dare bring up that kiss. This wasn't the time or place. Besides, he had the feeling they'd talked about it as much as they were going to when they'd danced around each other in the aftermath.

"You look great, too." She put a hand on her hip. "Who knew you had anything but jeans in your closet?"

"Doesn't everyone keep a surprise or two there?"

He grinned at her, and she tilted her glass in recognition of the insinuation.

"What I'm wondering, though," she said, "is what else you have tucked away, Liam."

He didn't tell her that she'd already pulled out his darkest skeleton. Sure, she had no idea how deep his hurt from the accident went, but there was no reason for her to know. Not with the rules she'd set down between them.

"You'd find my closet pretty boring," he said.

"Oh, come on. You can't entertain me with a juicy story like the one about Italy? Maybe something that explains how you turned out the way you did when you were raised in the heartland?"

"Ah, a story from my mad, bad youth." Funny how even though he and Jenny had spent a lot of time circling each other, they'd never gotten close enough to reveal more than where they'd come from geographically and superficially.

"I told you a little about my family," she said. "Time for you to tell me what yours is like."

She was raising her eyebrows, waiting, and maybe even hoping he'd refrain from talking about last night and instead go with this.

She had to know that he'd do anything for her.

So, naturally, he gave in. "Well, for starters, my parents chose to have only one kid—or maybe they predicted that I'd be enough to handle and they stopped there. But I have three uncles on my dad's side and four more aunts and uncles on my mom's, so any get-together was always a big, loud, Irish circus."

"And you were the most conservative of everyone, of course." She smiled to indicate her facetiousness.

"Hey, if you think I stood out, you should've met Uncle Tommy. They called him Tommy Pan, like Peter, except without the Lost Boys hanging around. About an hour into every gathering, he'd sneak off with me and a few of the other more adventurous cousins, and he'd pour us tiny highballs in the basement bar."

Jenny's mouth dropped open.

Liam held up his hands. "He didn't put much in each glass, just enough to make us feel like we were getting away with something. But Tommy…" He laughed. "Tommy's always been my favorite, and not only because he was a little nuts."

During his pause, he saw an expression on Jenny's face that seemed familiar, and he realized it was because she was fully locked onto every word he was saying.

Just as he was always locked onto her.

His heart seemed to twist around in his chest, as if it were trying to get out. But bit by bit, it relaxed, throbbing into a constant beat and clarifying his thoughts.

He and Jenny were incredibly in tune—more so than with any woman he'd ever met before.

Couldn't she see that?

Jenny reached out to touch his sleeve, bringing him back by creating a sizzle that rode his skin.

"Why's Tommy your favorite?" she asked. "Besides the highballs, I mean."

Liam smiled. "Because he'd do things that made my family throw up their hands and wonder what he could possibly be thinking. See, the McCrees are tidy, type-A small-towners who live comfortable lives, yet Tommy always pushed the envelope. He was in a Celtic rock band that toured the States until they went to the poorhouse. He went broke a second time when he invested in an environmentally beneficial green car that never made it past the planning stages. But Tommy didn't seem to care, because he was always his own man and he lived one hour at a time, enjoying what he called 'the days and nights of a lad who can be anything he wants to be.' So he inspired me to be the same way."

Especially after my accident changed the world as I knew it, Liam silently added.

Jenny's gaze had gone distant, and he knew something about his story had gotten to her.

Then she absently repeated, "Anything he wants to be."

And Liam knew.

He'd only told her about Tommy out of an effort to tame the awkwardness between them. But he realized that, once again, he'd managed to say what she needed to hear after losing her job…and her identity along with it.

The other day, he'd told her that she was valuable,

but could it be that he was valuable to her in some way, too?

"Where is Tommy now?" she asked.

"He fell madly in love with a sedate grade-school teacher," he said, hoping she'd note that Tommy had settled down with a woman who might've seemed all wrong for him once upon a time. "They got married and they now have four children he dotes on. But I'm pretty sure he's not giving them highballs in his basement."

When Jenny looked at him, he could see a question in her gaze.

And you, Liam? Are you ever going to stop wandering enough to turn out happy like Tommy?

Or maybe he was projecting his own questions onto her.

As Mei came over with his wine, he added one last thing.

"If there's hope for Tommy," he said, "there's hope for all of us."

Jenny's answering smile blinded him, and it was at that moment Liam finally stopped running from the truth.

He would stop wandering if she asked him to, because he was truly, undeniably in love with her.

Chapter Eight

The rest of Mei's get-together seemed to flash by for Jenny, but maybe that was because she hadn't strayed far from Liam the entire night.

As she'd expected, their constant conversation—the way they'd chatted with each other and no one else—had warranted a few interested glances from the other Sudsers who'd come and gone from the gathering. However, Jenny wasn't sure she cared all that much about causing whispers, even though it'd seemed like a bigger deal when she'd mentioned the possibility to Liam last night as they'd discussed the drawbacks of dating someone in the Club.

But the two of them weren't a couple, so why should it matter?

Or…

She thought of that kiss and how she was still obsessing about its tenderness.

Were they a couple and they just didn't know it?

The question stuck with her while they thanked and said goodbye to Mei and Travis at the door. Earlier, Jenny and Liam had gotten into an intense chat about traveling outside the United States versus inside it, only to be surprised to discover that they were the only ones left at the party, so they'd headed for the door quickly afterward.

Mei ran a gaze over Jenny's baggy-but-thin cardigan.

"It's getting cold out there," her friend said. "Do you want to borrow something thicker?"

"I'm five minutes away." Jenny hugged Mei and then stepped back into the hall. "I'll be fine."

"And if she changes her mind," Liam said, gesturing to the coat he'd already put on, "I've got it covered."

After Mei and Travis said their final farewells and shut the door, Jenny scanned Liam in his coat, which was black and came to his knees, almost like something out of the wild, wild west. She liked it because, coupled with his goatee, it gave him a gunfighter air.

In fact, she thought he looked pretty damned hot tonight.

As they made their way to the elevator, he favored his good leg. She'd seen the stiff way he moved earlier, too, but hadn't mentioned it because it looked as if he was downplaying his discomfort.

"That was fun," she said, pretending she didn't notice even now. "Was it worth missing happy hour for?"

The elevator doors slid open, and he extended his arm, inviting her to go inside the car first. He followed.

"Life is more than happy hours."

"Hey, I've met a few good dates during those. They can be useful every so often, even though they don't normally pay off in long-term dividends."

He laughed a little, shook his head, and pressed the button for the ground floor. The doors closed and the car eased downward.

"I think I know what you mean—how the places you meet people can be a good indicator of what might happen in the end," he said. "But I know plenty of couples who've turned happy hours into good relationships."

She thought about what a Laundromat might hold in store for two people, but that was so, so wrong.

Wasn't it?

She swallowed, her heart squeezing so tightly that it bumped up her pulse.

Or did she truly want Liam for herself?

Based on how close she felt to him right now, after a night when they'd chosen to spend every minute together to the exclusion of everyone else while locked in their own intimate bubble, she thought that wanting him was a perfectly natural thing.

So why shouldn't she give in to it? Why not put enough trust in herself to allow her feelings to guide her?

Her frenzied heartbeat took over her hearing, pulsating in her temples, her chest, and even low in the center of her, in a place she had believed was better left untouched before now....

The elevator opened in the lobby, and Liam had her exit before he did. Then, once they got to the main door, he opened it for her. She thanked him, then waited for him on the pavement. When he caught up to her, she took an automatic step back.

He flicked a glance at the space she'd left, as if to ask why it was needed.

Maybe because I'm nervous around you? she thought. *Because I'm afraid of what might happen if I kiss you again, and I'm doing everything within my power to resist it?*

She smiled at him, then started walking, hugging herself. The night air was rather nippy, yet somehow she felt warm inside.

But the uneven cadence of his steps consumed most of her attention.

She wanted to ask him if he needed to stop for a moment, but instead, she wandered over to a novelty shop window that featured Halloween costumes. If he needed to rest, there was no reason for her to spotlight it.

"Too cute," she said, pointing to a kid's version of a Captain Jack Sparrow getup, complete with scarf, dreadlocks and a plastic sword. "Can you imagine a bunch of pirates with eyeliner running around in a week or so?"

From behind her, his laugh caressed the back of her neck.

He obviously enjoyed the thought of kids at Halloween, and she recalled how natural he'd seemed with those Amati boys. They clearly adored him, and she couldn't help wondering if the notion of having a family had ever seized him.

She caught their reflection in the shop window: a man and a woman. She came up to his shoulder. The streetlamp shone over the lightness of her hair, which clashed with the darkness of his.

Opposites in so many ways except in the ones that seemed to matter the most lately.

Jenny shivered, not because she was cold, but because the image did something primal to her, creating brutal jabs low in her belly.

"You like kids, don't you, Liam?" she asked.

He'd started to take off his coat. "I like them well enough, I suppose."

"No, I'm talking about really like. When you were with those Amati boys, I saw it. You were relaxed around them. You genuinely enjoy being with them."

"Maybe that's just because they're the Amati boys. Who can resist two such funny little goofballs?"

He slipped his coat over Jenny's shoulders, and her body flooded with heat. He'd seen her shiver, and he'd come to her aid without even hesitating. Little did he know that she'd only been trembling because he was standing right here, close enough so that she could smell his cedar scent, so that she didn't have to do much to imagine what his skin would feel like against hers.

God, she really did want Liam.

Terribly.

Achingly.

But what if she couldn't handle the emotions he brought with him?

Or, worse yet, what if the two of them did start something up and he ultimately left her because he couldn't handle the strain of what her future might hold?

She thanked him once again while pushing her arms

through the coat, cuddling into it and moving away from the window. Her belly trembled, because the wool smelled fresh and clean like him.

"I can give this back to you tomorrow," she said.

"Or you can give it back when we get to your place."

She should've known that he would escort her home, although Placid Valley was as safe as you could get, even at night.

"Liam?" she asked as they continued walking.

He sighed melodramatically. "What sort of loaded question do you plan on posing to me now?"

She smiled at him. "You always say that you're not good at relationships, but for the life of me, I can't understand why that is. Not when you know when to put a coat around a girl's shoulders or when you seem to have the instincts of a gentleman."

"I was raised to open doors for others. Besides, being a gentleman is a lot less work than maintaining an actual relationship."

The sound of him laboring to walk got to her, and she slowed even more, but not enough to make it obvious. "Why does it take so much work for *you?*"

He must've heard the sincere curiosity in her voice, because she really couldn't figure out why a woman hadn't snapped up Liam long ago.

He seemed to think about her question for a while, and when he answered, she sensed that he wasn't being entirely straightforward.

"I find it hard to devote myself to both a woman and a career," he said. "Developing a business takes a great deal of my attention and devotion, and the women I've dated think that what I'm trying to accomplish is great…for a short time. Then they lose patience."

"Are you telling me that once you get serious with a woman, you neglect her in favor of your work? Is that why relationships are so hard?"

He wasn't looking at her, and now she really wondered if he was only making up excuses for something that ran much deeper.

She narrowed her eyes at him. "I think there's way more to it, Liam."

He ran a hand through his hair, then shook his head, as if he knew he wasn't going to get around explaining to her. "Maybe I just can't move forward in some ways, even though I'm trying my best with the business."

His candor gave her pause. She had a feeling that he was talking about his accident and how it had done more to him than merely affect his body. It'd done some damage down deep, hadn't it? She should've known from that day he'd told her about it—he'd been so nonchalant about the story.

"Your injury interferes with relationships, too?" she asked softly.

He kept moving forward, as if stopping was unthinkable now.

"You know about my scars," he said. "And until a person sees them, they say that there's no way the injuries can be ugly or unnerving. Then they get a good look."

She couldn't believe it was that simple. Maybe the scarring went far below the skin and the discomfort carried over into how he related to others.

The more she thought about Liam sitting in the Laundromat corner, the more she started to understand. Still, how could scars really have enough of an effect to harm a relationship?

Her question whipped around and came right back at her. Hadn't she been just as afraid of what would be left of her after the biopsy, even though she'd been told that the small scar would fade with time?

But how about after a lumpectomy or mastectomy?

A tiny voice echoed in the back of her mind. *If you're making the assumption that physical changes don't have much of an effect on how others see a person, Jenny, then why are you so afraid?*

Yet as they closed in on her apartment building, she knew that she was only scratching the surface of the issue. She was afraid of being damaged in a much more profound way.

In the soul, where a person kept their dreams.

When they stopped at her gate, she faced him.

"Why do you think those women shied away from your wound?" she asked gently, hoping she wasn't going too far. If she was, she'd put an end to the conversation.

"Listen, it wasn't because of the scars themselves," he said, his voice taut. He was talking around the subject of the women. "It's more about not living up to an ideal that someone has of you."

"You think because you're wounded, you're not as much of a man to others?"

And did she think that she might not be as much of a woman in the future…?

"Maybe it's not about being a man," he said, sighing. "Maybe it's just about losing something that was a part of you, and now you're never going to be that complete person you thought you'd be." He stuck his hands in his pockets. "I think the biggest scar of all comes when there's pity on the face of someone you started to give your heart to."

She was going to pursue that tidbit later, but hearing him talk about his own fears put things into perspective for her now; she wanted to tell him that she didn't see him as a wounded person at all. That there was so much more to him than this label.

Yet how could she comfort him by saying that one truth existed for him and the same truth didn't exist for her? Why would his misfortunes not matter though hers would?

He seemed to realize that he was chiseling away at her in some way, and he touched her arm.

"I've been talking too much."

"No, I appreciate your honesty." She took hold of his hand. "More than you know."

The feel of his skin set her veins vibrating, and when she unlocked the gate, she kept a grip on his hand, not wanting him to leave, feeling closer to him than she'd ever thought possible.

Feeling him.

"Why don't you come inside for a bit?" she asked.

He looked tempted and wary at the same time, and she knew it was because they'd gotten into some heavy stuff and he probably didn't wish to go any further.

But she truly didn't want him to go.

In fact, that impulsive side of her that'd kissed him last night wanted to prove to him, as well as to herself, that damage didn't and wouldn't matter.

Her adrenaline took over, giving her crazy ideas, pumping her body with such a need for him that she had to slow her steps as she led him to her door.

Once there, she unlocked it.

Liam came inside, still cursing himself for getting so swept up in confiding in Jenny that he'd left behind his excuses about work affecting his relationships and then gone on to reveal how his scars had marked his life instead. It was just that he and Jenny had interacted so easily, so perfectly, the entire night that he'd just about forgotten who he was talking to—a woman who might be about to undergo her own round of scars.

Still, Jenny hadn't withdrawn at his frank revelations. In fact, she was even now sitting him down on the very couch he'd reclined on last week, back when they hadn't even known how to communicate without teasing each other.

"What can I get for you?" she asked.

"Nothing."

"Juice, water, tea?"

"Sounds like you're going to nurse me."

There was an edge to his words, his defenses rising because he'd be damned if he let her in farther than she'd already gotten.

But wasn't that what he wanted? For her to get closer?

No. Loving her in silence was one thing; the whole "I don't want a boyfriend" stance she'd embraced had given him some room to feel.

But he hadn't expected her to pursue his deep, dark secrets and for him to give in to her.

Had he only admitted his feelings to himself earlier tonight because he'd surmised that she was safe to love from a near distance?

Well, she wasn't so safe anymore, was she?

While he tried to decide whether he should leave—he could go just as soon as his leg stopped being difficult—she went to the entry closet, leaving his blood to pound in his ears.

Soon enough, she was back, having shed his large coat to showcase that baggy sweater.

Then Jenny sat next to him and he stiffened—and not just through his shoulders and back. His body had been primed for her all night, and with her inches away, he could barely take it.

She rested a hand near his thigh, and he almost hit the roof.

"Feel better?" she asked.

He cleared his throat. "Yeah."

She hesitated, then touched the side of his leg, near his knee.

It warmed his whole limb, spreading darts of sensation to his groin, too.

"Careful, Jenny," he said, his voice gritty.

"That's what I've been telling myself, too."

Yet in spite of that, she slid her hand up to his knee, as if intending to massage it, and he instinctively stifled a groan. He reached down to move her hand away, but she threaded her fingers through his instead.

"You want to see the scars," he said. "That's what this is about. It's a challenge for you now."

"Don't think that way," she said softly. "I'm just

wondering how many women could have possibly had a bad reaction when they saw your leg. Was it just one? And did she mean so much to you that her response made you defensive?"

"It only took one reaction." He girded himself, even though he was on fire. "And, yes, she was an actual girl-friend, not a fling. So I learned from it, loud and clear."

"Not everyone will be like her." She tightened her grip on his hand.

Liam stayed wary, because it seemed that Jenny had decided to prove something, and he was pretty sure it had to do with withstanding the sight of his damage so she could strengthen herself for the possibility of her own.

And he wanted to give that to her. More than any-thing, he did. But Liam had kept himself covered around women for years: he'd used sheets and darkness and lack of true intimacy to refrain from feeling like some-one they needed to feel sorry for. He couldn't stand the thought of Jenny patronizing him, too, so he guided her hand away from his leg.

Yet she wasn't letting him off the hook that easily.

"I hate seeing you sad," she said. Then she lowered her tone, and it rocked him with its urgency, with its note of yearning.

"Liam."

She rested her fingertips on his cheek, stroking down to his chin, then to his bottom lip. He sucked in breath, wanting her so damned badly, but unwilling to expose what he'd tried so hard to hide.

Before he knew it, she'd leaned forward to kiss him,

and all his walls crashed down, blinding him with the dust of their fall.

Unlike their first kiss, this one was harder, more demanding as she buried a hand in his hair and tugged him closer. A ferocious longing fireworked through him, and he scooped her up in one arm to bring her halfway onto his lap.

As if she'd let go of all control herself, she slid the rest of the way over him, straddling him, resting much of her weight on his left side in deference to his sore leg. Then she skimmed her hand down his chest, her fingertips spiking him with electric sensation as she explored him, then coasted her hand over his ribs and to his back.

At the same time, her other hand kept gripping his hair while her mouth sucked at his, drawing them into a warm, moist, lazy cadence.

Getting in too deep, he thought.

Loving her was one thing, but baring himself to her was another.

Yet that was a part of love, wasn't it? So how could he avoid it?

His body wouldn't allow him to argue as they kissed and kissed, as he reached in back of and beneath her sweater to glide his fingers down her spine. She quivered, and he continued, mapping the beautiful, full curves of her waist, her hips.

His pulse took him over while he traced over her ribs.

He'd been hoping for this all night, and he knew she had been, too.

But what about more than a kiss?

His thumb brushed the underside of her breast, and she broke away from him, holding hands with him again while panting and shifting on his lap to bring herself even closer.

She'd been afraid for him to touch her there, he thought, and he should've anticipated that, but his head had been too clouded. And as her skirt rode to the middle of her thighs, making him hotter, more excited, he tried to keep her best interests at the front of his every speeding thought, his every hot-blooded action.

"Here, Liam," she whispered against his mouth, leading his hands to the sides of her thighs. "Why don't you touch me here?"

Instead of the other place you wanted to touch.

Yeah, she definitely had something to prove, and she was going fast—as if she were racing to get to a finish line that would provide some kind of knowledge as a prize. But he found himself all too willing to help her, and he worshipfully ran his thumbs between her knees, savoring her lush skin before he went any higher, as his libido was begging him to do.

Jenny, his greatest dream...

She bit her lip, then scooted forward another inch or two on his lap and wrapped her arms around his shoulders and head for an even deeper kiss. They parted their lips, slowing the pace but also heightening the intensity. He slid his tongue into her mouth and she met him with deliberate, sensual strokes.

They devoured each other, as if enjoying each taste, each suck. His growing erection strained against his fly, and she separated her legs even more, easing down to him until the center of her brushed him.

He moaned, and she used one of her hands to work open the rest of his shirt. She reached her hand inside, skimming her fingertips down his chest, his stomach, until he bucked against her. She answered by shifting her hips again and making full contact with his arousal. This time, she made a pleasured sound as she leaned her head back, her neck arched.

Desire speared him, goading him to push her hips forward so his tip pressed against her.

"Liam," she said on a groan.

She ground into him harder, and he needed no further invitation.

He moved her off his lap and laid her on the couch, poising himself over her as he slipped off her pumps and dropped them to the floor.

From their movements, her skirt had ridden up, and as she left it the way it was, he could see the unfocused lust in her eyes, the continuation of the experimentation she was embarking upon, the impetuousness she'd admitted to when she'd started that kiss last night.

The hunger for an intimacy she hadn't experienced since her breakup with that boyfriend.

And she had chosen Liam to give it to her, yet not in the way she might want. He couldn't strip down until every inch of skin showed.

He wouldn't.

But he would make her feel as good as he could.

He felt his leg twinge, and he changed position, taking the weight off it while he shucked off his shirt. When he was finished, the famished appreciation in her gaze made his pulse bang until his body was one big throb.

She reached up, touched his chest, then trailed her hand down and down until she hitched her fingers into his waistband, her nails skimming his belly.

They were at the edge of a cliff, he thought. A point where they could never go back.

And when she stroked over his arousal, he dove head-first, his body clutching in its swan dive deeper and deeper into her, his hand covering hers.

"How far do you want this to go?" he asked in a strained tone.

"As far as we want it to."

But from the way she had directed him away from her breast earlier, he knew it wasn't going to go far enough.

For either of them.

With the same daredevil need in her gaze, she watched him while reaching under her skirt to hook her thumbs into her lace panties.

"Jenny…" A warning tone, telling her that if she continued, it'd be hell for him to stop. It'd be hard enough anyway at this point.

"This is something I haven't wanted to do with any other man in a long time," she said. "But I'm ready now. So damned ready, Liam."

When she began to pull her panties down, it was beyond him to do anything but help her to work them off her legs, then discard them.

And there she was, a part of his fantasy, inviting him into reality.

Taking care, he rested a hand on her thigh, then slid it higher as she arched her back, anticipating him.

The second he touched her—so hot, so ready—she

took in a sharp breath. Driven, he rubbed his thumb into her folds, and she reached behind her to grab the couch's wooden armrest.

"Yes," she whispered, burying her flushed face against her arm. The sweater covered half of her ecstatic expression.

He slid his thumb to the most sensitive part of her, then circled it. Her hips took up his motions, churning.

"Liam."

His name was a stronger urging from her now, and he eased a finger inside her.

She wrapped a leg around him, bracing her other foot on the carpet. The carnal sight of her so open for him sent his vision to a red, beating haze that melted down his body until it joined with the fierce pounding between his legs.

He stroked a second finger into her.

With little cries of delight, she met his thrusts, and his vision deepened to a thicker, all-consuming crimson.

As he pleasured her, as her gasps got faster, louder, she reached up to pull him down for another kiss while her hips rocked up to him again.

"Protection?" she whispered in his ear. "I'm not on the pill anymore. Do you…?"

Damn it.

He removed his fingers from her, fumbled for his pants, got a condom out of his pocket, then worked on getting himself sheathed.

Meanwhile, Jenny panted, and when he was ready he paused, willing to do anything for her, even stop right now by using every ounce of strength he had left.

But she grasped him, pulling him forward, and he slid into her with one thrust.

She dug her fingers into his bare back, sounds of incredible bliss in his ear as he drove into her, pounded into her, until his reddened sight went dark.

But then, in the pulsing of his thoughts, he pictured Jenny in the darkness of his closed eyes.

A flash of her.

Another heartbeatlike peek.

A faster one.

Another.

She filled his vision, banging through him, coming faster, faster, faster—

He exploded as she raised her hips and gave a cry of release, too, and he buried his face in her neck, consumed by her musky, clover-laden scent.

Their breathing traded rhythms—her chest expanding while his fell, as if they were trying to match each other but they were just a beat off.

Gradually, he realized that his bare chest was against her clothed one, and that she was uncovered below while he was covered except for where he rested inside her.

And that, in turn, made him realize that they were still two strangers, albeit ones who had reached out to each other to test what was beneath the layers that they hadn't been able to shed.

That wasn't good enough for Liam anymore.

He wanted to uncover more of himself, even if it wasn't what she'd initially tried to coax out of him.

He'd give her what he could by telling her what he knew about her secret.

Chapter Nine

Even now, an hour after they'd made love, an hour after they'd gotten themselves back together and then returned to the couch to just quietly lie in each other's arms, Jenny's skin was still sensitized. Her body and spirits still on a mind-scrambling high.

She rested her head against Liam's chest, her hand on top of his heart while she gauged the soft, rhythmic patter of his pulse and wondered if he'd fallen asleep.

It didn't much matter, though, because she was happy like this, one of her legs between his, his hand nestled against the small of her back.

Happier than she'd ever predicted.

She'd made the right choice, even though it'd been one she would've hesitated to make as the old Jenny.

If she had felt close to him earlier in the night, she

definitely was a full part of him now. He'd been inside her, and not just physically; their lovemaking had meant so much more, and now Jenny knew the difference between this and the other sex she'd had.

Being with a man should transcend want or need— it was something to treasure with a partner who touched you truly and deeply. She tried to put a name to what she was feeling, but the force of her emotions caused a guardian—an inner protector—to come out.

How can you afford to be thinking about deep feelings for him right now? it asked. *The consequences could be too overwhelming and even destructive.*

Besides, it added, she had only been balancing on an emotional tightrope lately, and once morning came, she would realize that she was misinterpreting the connection she'd experienced with him.

Yet if this feeling wasn't a bigger emotion than she'd ever felt before, why had she wanted all of him?

Her guardian spun out answers: Maybe she had seduced him because she'd wanted to make him feel better. Maybe their union had come out of some kind of pity she might've felt after he'd told her about his reasons for never committing.

But when she thought about how they'd touched, how he'd moved her, the adrenaline threaded through her again, stringing her together with a pumping yearning.

As well as trepidation.

She realized her mouth was dry, and she decided she needed a glass of water. Quietly, she got up, careful not to wake him. Then, once on her bare feet, she smoothed her dress and looked down at Liam, who still had his sleep-relaxed hand over the spot she'd just deserted, as if he were even now holding her.

Affection needled her heart and she took a lung-filling breath.

What now?

Had she opened a door to trouble with her damned impulses?

Crossing her arms over her chest, she went to the kitchen, then poured herself and Liam some water from the dispenser in her refrigerator. She padded back to the living room, only to find him propped on his elbows, his body long and lean on her couch, his face warmed from slumber. But he had this look on his face—a combination of being glad to see her, of desiring her again, and of wondering if she would tell him it'd all been a mistake.

Her stomach turned upside down, and she didn't know if it was because she wasn't sure about the mistake part, or if it was because *she* wanted *him* again.

"Morning," he said.

"Not yet." She gestured with one of the glasses to the digital time on her TV's DVR unit. "It's just past the stroke of midnight."

"Feels like the sun's up."

He grinned, and now her heart did a tumbling act, too.

She smiled back, almost shyly, which was odd since she'd felt very much in control earlier. To break the tension, she put their glasses down on the coffee table, then changed her mind and held on to hers, just to keep something in her hands.

He sat up.

She sat down.

"How's your leg?" she asked.

"Still singing off tune."

He scooted toward the edge of the couch, almost as if he were intending to leave.

So soon?

The lightness in her stomach went heavy, and that guardian told her that she shouldn't have hoped for any other outcome but this. Tonight had been a mistake between two friends, it continued, and the sooner she and Liam admitted that, the better.

He'd turned toward her, and she could tell that he was struggling with whatever it was he needed to say. She braced herself.

"There's something I've been meaning to talk to you about," he said, "and I don't feel right about keeping it back anymore. But the thing is, I know telling you is going to throw a real wrench into everything."

She didn't want to hear this. Couldn't they avoid reality for a little longer?

Couldn't they just go back to kissing?

He read her silence and touched her arm. Her skin came alive, just as it always did with him.

"I've never been this emotional with a woman," he said. "I've never…"

He trailed off, and Jenny looked into his eyes. They were steeped in something she'd never recognized in a man before—something that was tearing him apart even while linking him to her.

Love?

The hope—and the fear—shook her, rattling her foundations.

Love could be broken if too much weight was put on it—like the weight *she* was carrying around with her.

Now he rested his fingertips against her cheek. "I know what's been bothering you."

Her vision seemed to go lopsided. "You...know?"

God, why was she playing dumb when she'd always suspected that he'd overheard her in the Laundromat that day?

Because that was what he was referring to, wasn't it?

His hand trailed to her jaw, where he cupped her with his palm.

"I caught you and Mei talking, and I've kept it to myself ever since. But I've seen how the news has been eating away at you, and it's been doing the same to me."

She shook her head, and he dropped his hand away from her.

"You know, I had a feeling you overheard," she said, "but I wish you hadn't said anything. I wish we could've kept going along without ever directly talking about it."

"I'm sorry, Jenny."

"No, you shouldn't be sorry." Her breath hitched. "I took comfort from the assurance that you still treated me the same, even if you knew. I told myself that you were the only one who looked at me the same way you always had. Whenever I was around you, I could fool myself into thinking nothing had changed or was going to change about who I was." Drained, she slumped. "But avoiding the issue isn't going to make what you heard go away like that."

"I wish I could do something to make it go away."

Wet heat started to fill her eyes, but she wouldn't cry, even though her throat and chest had gone tight.

"You tried," she said, setting her water glass on the coffee table. The liquid sloshed, messy, just like her life had become.

"You made me smile when I thought I wouldn't be able to do it ever again," she said. "You still saw the old Jenny—the woman who hadn't changed. And you liked her."

"I've always liked her, and I always will."

His gaze told her that "like" wasn't nearly enough to communicate what he really felt, and she was afraid he'd take that next step and turn "like" into "love." It seemed he was a little reluctant to go there, too, because he returned to the original point.

Thank goodness.

But that didn't stop disappointment from jabbing her gut.

"I'm never going to tell a soul about what I found out," he said. "Believe that. But I also want you to know that if you need it, you've got a lot of people who would drop everything to support you and help you face what might be ahead. If you'd allow it."

She started to fold her arms over her chest again, but he put a halt to that.

"Jenny."

His tone was gentle yet no-nonsense, and she only made it halfway into her self-imposed shelter.

"You're independent to the bone," he said, "but reaching out to others for help wouldn't change your ability to be the strong woman you've always been."

"You don't think so?" The sting in her throat made it hard to talk. "Because I'm afraid a bad-news diagnosis will change a lot of things, including that, McCree."

He flinched slightly at the use of his last name, and she hated that it had slipped out, especially after tonight's soul-wrapping intimacy.

But maybe that was why she'd said it—to push him back to the fringes, where she wouldn't have to bother him with her issues or mortify herself if she ended up getting sick.

"You told me earlier about your accident," she said, "and even though you said that you felt like less of a *person* and not like less of a man, I do feel as if that personal, and physical, part of my own self might be disappearing."

Her femininity.

Maybe that was the reason she'd made love so easily and arduously with Liam tonight.

But it had paid off, because he'd shown her that she wasn't lacking, even if she had kept part of herself covered from him.

A tear slid down her face, and she wiped it away. She hadn't meant to admit all this out loud.

He didn't touch her again, probably because her body language told him not to. But his voice was just as much of a soothing caress.

"Can't you see that, no matter what, you're perfect, Jenny?" he asked. "Nothing, absolutely *nothing,* is going to make that different."

He spoke with such conviction that her tears came harder.

"You say that now, but what happens down the road if I'm not cleared?"

"I'll probably say that you're the bravest woman I know, and I'd be damned lucky to be with that woman."

He had no idea what he was saying. But he went on, yanking at her heartstrings and at her will to keep herself removed and safe.

"Maybe you'll get good news," he said. "But if it happens that you don't, I realize what I'm getting into here. I knew it before we even kissed, for God's sake. And I've even been wondering if you were going to reject me first."

But even though she could see beyond his injuries, she still couldn't reconcile how he would be able to get beyond hers.

"Maybe neither of us was made to be intimate," she said.

"Or maybe we were made for each other."

His statement fed the blazing flame that had been burning in the bleakest part of her.

Made for each other. If only that were true.

He leaned nearer, and she didn't move away this time.

"I'll be there for you," he said. "In hindsight, I wish I'd allowed someone to help me more after my accident, but I didn't. I fought my parents every time they took me to therapy, and I didn't let them support me in the aftermath. I didn't let anyone close enough to even try because I was so bitter at what I'd lost. It took years for me to come around, and that was so unnecessary."

As he wiped the tears from her face, she saw the man he was: the wounded, disappointed boy who'd learned from life and become a wandering free spirit who didn't open his heart as easily as he used to.

Until now, with her.

But in spite of his optimism, he really didn't know what he might be up against, and seeing his promises disappear when reality hit would hurt them both.

Yet she should've thought of that before they'd made love, she mused, drawing her sweater around her like the most dependable ally she had.

She should've thought of it before she'd started falling for him, too.

The minute Liam saw Jenny withdrawing, he was pretty sure he'd been right about the reason she'd initiated their lovemaking, whether she knew it or not.

She'd done it to try to figure out what she was still about, how she still fit into her own image of herself.

And telling her that he knew her secret had only pushed her away.

Sitting here on the couch, where they'd joined earlier in such pure emotion, where nothing from the outside world had touched them, he didn't know what to do.

Stay?

Go?

All he knew was that if he walked out that door right now, he might never recover, because Jenny was the one for him.

He'd known it the first time he'd seen her.

As he weighed the ramifications of staying, going, Jenny gave him a tentative smile.

"I hope you're going to stay, Liam." Then she threw

in a half-teasing capper, as if she were desperate to lighten the mood. "I'll be damned if you're going to walk home on that leg right now."

Truthfully, it wasn't his first choice, either, but when she got up from the couch, opened a wooden chest in a corner, pulled out a blanket, then walked back over and laid it on his lap, his chest seemed to crack open.

In her own way, she was letting him know that keeping him from walking home was merely an excuse to have him around, even if she still looked confused about what she truly wanted.

That decided it for him.

He wasn't going anywhere, mostly because the only place he longed to be was here, but also because his leaving might make her think that he was abandoning her, which was the last thing he ever intended to do.

He leaned back his head and rested it on the couch, getting comfortable. She looked content at that, and her expression made him feel the same way.

She drank her water as he pulled the blanket over himself and closed his eyes, reveling in the nearness of her as she sank against the cushions next to him when she'd finished.

He must've fallen asleep not long after that, because in what seemed like the next instant, he woke up to find himself in the same position, but with Jenny's head on his shoulder and the blanket covering both of them.

Before she awakened, too, he touched her blond hair, and a slam of affection vibrated within him.

I'll be there for you, he'd said.

The contact roused her, and with a long inhalation, she rubbed her cheek against his shoulder, then peered up at him with eyes slightly swollen from her crying.

Yet she looked as beautiful as ever to him.

Both of them just stared at each other until she sat up and he noticed that she wasn't wearing the sweater. Her dress wasn't exactly snug, but…

No sweater.

He smiled to himself, running a hand over his face so she wouldn't see how the tiny detail got to him.

"Now it's morning," she said, gesturing toward the DVR clock, which read 7:07.

He rubbed the back of his neck, feeling the effects of sleeping upright on the couch. "I suppose I should get going."

"Do you have big plans for a Saturday?"

"Not much more than the ordinary, which means that I'm going to watch some college football and get some hoops in later with the guys after working a little."

"How about breakfast to prepare you for all that activity?"

She stood, and he almost thought life was back to normal, except for the trace of tension in the air.

"For someone who doesn't cook much," he said, "you sure do provide."

"Oh, a bagel in the toaster, some cream cheese on top…hardly gourmet. I don't drink coffee, though, so if you're a caffeine addict you're out of luck. But I've got orange and apple juice."

"Orange is good."

She took off, just like the got-to-be-doing-something

Jenny he'd always known. But she was a little more fidgety this morning.

Big wonder why.

He got up, rubbing his leg, then followed to lean against the wall while she made quick work out of slicing the bagels and putting them into her toaster.

So what was their status now? he wondered.

A couple?

Not a couple?

She poured them some juice. "I was wondering about something, Liam."

Okay. Here it went. But at least they were back to first names.

"You're always wondering something," he said.

She grinned at him while handing over the glass of juice. "I never got around to asking this last night, what with the way things…heated up."

Her gaze caught his, and he nearly imploded. But then she blushed a wild pink, looked away, and Liam guessed that she was willing to acknowledge the sex but not what he'd brought up afterward.

Had revealing that he'd known about her secret been the main reason for this friendly yet far less loving cool-off? Had his knowledge been even more intimate than the sex itself, and was she having trouble handling that?

Who knew, but he was glad he'd put her secret out in the open.

"So what were you going to ask me before the heat got to us?" he asked.

She fetched the bagels that had popped out of the

toaster. "It's about your work. How close are you to really busting out with your company?"

Was she interested?

"The bank loan should be coming through soon, so I'll be able to expand then. Right now, though, I've got a small but strong list of clients, and I've improved their Web presence, which makes for a good start. But if I'm going to get to the next level, I need to hire employees to design business plans, marketing strategies and infrastructure details."

She used a knife to smooth cream cheese over a bagel. "And McCree and Associates…is it going to offer things like insurance and benefits to the employees?"

He leaned on the counter. Was she hinting about coming on board?

"If I want to attract the best," he said, "I have to offer the best. And I already have a couple of college buddies who want to consult with me." He raised an eyebrow. "Why do you ask?"

"Maybe because I never asked before."

She smiled at him, her hair tousled from sleep. The rumpled sight screwed into him, because he'd helped to make that hair messy.

"Not that you've committed to anything at all," he said, "but have you thought about the consequences of working with me?"

"We can separate business and…"

Pleasure? he finished for her in his head.

Or business and friendship?

He'd promised her that he would always be around, and that included being anything she needed—lover or friend. Even though he hoped it was the former, that hidden, protected portion of him that had been so hurt in the past was fine with remaining covered under the cloak of friendship.

He took the pressure off her to define what they were to each other now.

"Listen, Jenny—think long and hard about what you want to do with your talents now that you're not with Kendrick Corporation anymore. I'm sure you'll have recruiters knocking at your door from some tempting places."

"Hasn't happened yet."

"You just wait."

"Thanks for saying so."

"Hey," he said, making her pause in her breakfast efforts. "I'm not tossing out platitudes. As a matter of fact, I was thinking that you might even consider floating me some ideas for my Web site on a consulting basis—without going against your separation agreement and revealing trade secrets from Kendrick, of course." He grinned. "I haven't been able to hit the right note with it."

She laughed, as if still thinking he was just doing this to patronize her. But then she saw how serious he was, and the laughter faded.

"Okay," she said, smiling, her gaze going soft. "I'd really like that, Liam. Thanks for the offer."

"No, thank *you*."

The sound of more laughter, appreciative this time, was like a gush of refreshing water over him. But he wondered if that was how she was going to think of him from this point on—as a person to lean on, not a man who just might be willing to put himself out on an emotional limb if she'd only let him.

Jenny and Liam ended up going to his apartment, to his secondary office, where he'd left his computer. There, he explained his own business plan and showed her around the initial version of his Web site.

As the day flowed on, Jenny stayed at his apartment, although she told herself that maybe it would be a good idea to put some distance between them, to get some perspective. Maybe that was only because she was so on pins and needles about Wednesday, when she would visit the outpatient clinic for the procedure that would tell her how worried she should be about her lump.

Nonetheless, she liked being at his place for the time being, sitting in a tattered recliner that had been used enough to feel cozy. But his apartment wasn't exactly designed to encourage hominess—Liam clearly traveled light, even when he was settled. This studio, with the showpiece of a black futon, a TV on a former kitchen table and a lone floor lamp hovering over the paper-strewn computer station, testified to that. The only sign of collecting was a shelf full of vinyl records—hundreds of them—and Jenny wondered why those held such appeal for Liam.

She would ask later, because she was presently sketching ideas for a new logo for his company—her idea, not his—while keeping an eye on a Kansas Jayhawks football game. At the same time, a constant kick of anxiety was also causing her to fidget. In fact, she was wiggling her foot when Liam caught her for about the fiftieth time.

"You're squirming enough to power an entire community," he said jokingly.

"Sorry."

She tucked her feet under her, glancing at him splayed out on the futon—the traditional male pigskin-watching position. From her spot on the chair, it seemed like he was a chasm away instead of merely feet, and she wished she could just listen to her instincts and sit next to him, his arm brushing against hers, his scent filling her up.

She was still in a lengthened afterglow stage after last night, her body pulling toward his. But though he was obviously waiting for her to make another move, it wouldn't be nice to keep taking from him when she could only give so much right now.

The Jayhawks called a time-out, and Liam put the game on mute. "So what've you got?"

She held up her sketch, with its twined design that incorporated both the name of his company and a feeling of synergy. He'd insisted on paying for her time in creating the graphic, but she was only helping and didn't intend to accept a dime. Not unless she joined his team—an idea that had just started to solidify in the past few days. Too bad it'd taken getting laid off for her to consider it, but even with this tiny project, she felt so much freer than she had in years.

He smiled at her work. "That looks great."

Great. Humph.

"But…it's not quite what you envisioned?" She put the pad on her lap and inspected it for flaws. "I can modify. Just tell me what you need."

"No, I meant what I said. It's great." He smiled, almost as if to himself. "I knew you'd be the one who could put some zing into it."

Was he giving her a load of sweet talk?

No, there was a genuine respect in his voice that she couldn't deny.

Then again, he'd always sounded that way with her, even the first time he'd offered her a job.

She gave him a look from beneath her lashes. A prince in disguise, she thought. Why hadn't she ever seen it?

He'd turned the TV's sound back on, and she tried to concentrate on the logo, but thoughts of Wednesday got to her again, and she started to wiggle her foot.

Liam glanced at her, his eyes telling her that he knew why she couldn't calm down. Then he gestured for her to sit next to him on the futon.

How could she resist?

Even though she knew she should be keeping a couple of feet between them at all times unless she wanted a repeat of last night, she eased onto the couch and cuddled against him.

He put his arm around her in what seemed like a casual embrace. Yet she could feel the beat of attraction pounding between them.

Resist, she thought. *Must...resist....*

But her emotions took over, and she went with her gut, just as she'd been doing too much lately.

"Liam?" she asked over the cheering of the game.

"Uh-oh, another 'I was wondering' question?"

Her heartbeat raced as she kept her gaze glued to the security of the TV. "You can say no if you want, but

Wednesday, would you…drive me to my biopsy appointment? I mean, you're one of the few who knows what's going on, and Mei has her daughter to take care of, and I know having to chauffeur me around would disrupt her day. Of course, it'd disrupt yours, too…."

His arm tightened around her, as if he hadn't expected her to ask.

"I know it's a big favor," she added, "but I'll be under a local anesthetic and sedative, so they recommend that I have someone drive me back home. I just thought I might ask…you."

She held her breath, having chosen him to do so much more than just transport her back and forth to an appointment. She was trusting him, reaching out to him like he'd asked her to.

Was he wondering why she'd invited him into this part of her life?

It was a good question.

Why?

Did she even have any right to ask him?

But true to form, he put an end to her worries.

"I told you before," he said softly—but firmly. "I'll be there."

Although she kept telling herself that his promises would stop coming soon, she slipped her arm through his, taking him while she could.

Chapter Ten

When night shaded Liam's windows, Jenny was still at his apartment, working away at his computer to type up all the ideas she'd hatched during their day together. Not that he minded having her here. At all. But he saw her pushing herself, as if driving the demons out, and he knew it wasn't going to do her any good. She wasn't going to forget about the appointment, and seeing her trying so hard to do so disturbed him.

"Jenny," he finally said when eight o'clock rolled around. "All work and no play make for an evening that I'd rather spend in the city listening to a band in a club or eating Italian pastry in North Beach."

She glanced up from the keyboard, as if time had held no meaning for her. He pointed to the old clock he'd hung over the computer station.

When she saw the time, she leaned back in the chair and rubbed her eyes. "I was on a roll."

"So this is what you want to keep doing all night?" he asked. "Work?"

She got a look on her face that told him she wasn't sure what other activities he might have in mind. Then he saw a flash of remembrance in her gaze: last night. Making love with him.

Had she found something new within herself when she was with him, just as he did whenever he was with her? Had she seen a different person—one she hadn't ever thought existed?

Maybe Liam was hoping that he had been enough to persuade her that she didn't *have* to redefine herself in the face of a crisis; she could still be Jenny and come out victorious in whatever she did.

"Well, then," he said, catching her attention again, "if you plan to keep on laboring the night away, I've got an even more challenging task for you."

She almost looked relieved for a further opportunity to be Go-Get-'Em Jenny, the woman who clearly used work as a life eraser.

"Does it have to do with creating more graphics?" she asked.

"It's image related, all right." He rose from the futon, where he'd been reading the latest issue of *Wired* magazine while waiting for her to run out of fuel.

Which had never happened.

Then he strolled over to the darkened TV, which cast a faint reflection back at him. Stroking the slight goatee on his chin, he said, "I'm making over McCree and Associates, so I suppose the McCree part needs to catch up to its new, professional look along with everything else."

In the TV, he caught a glimpse of her in back of him, sitting forward in her chair.

There, he thought, his heart jumping. *That's the Jenny I like to see.*

"Are you saying what I think you're saying?" she asked.

"The goatee's history."

She laughed in apparent disbelief. "Are you sure about that? I mean, it's so…you, Liam. I'm not sure I'll even know you without it."

He turned around. "Yes, you will."

From the softening of her eyes, he could see that she got it: what mattered wasn't on the surface.

Not with either of them.

He even thought he might be ready to put his money where his mouth was: to trust Jenny enough to let her see all of him as he uncovered himself bit by bit, starting with this small gesture.

She rose from the chair and came out from behind the table, and his nerves sang.

But so did his heart.

"I get the honor of doing the shaving?" she asked.

"I wouldn't leave it to anyone else."

"And I get to go through your closet? And give your hair a trim?"

Whoa—he'd created a monster here. "One thing at a time, okay?"

When she laughed like a naughty minx and headed for the lone closet in his studio, Liam allowed himself a moment of appreciating her verve. It'd always drawn him to her, and to see it in full light now did things to him that he'd never thought possible.

Hearts and flowers, love notes and ballads…he'd always thought them corny, but now they made perfect sense.

She found a garment bag in the depths of his closet and unzipped it to find a dark gray business suit inside. "Well, look here."

"Never worn it," he said, coming closer. When he stood next to her, a force field of energy seemed to pull him in. "It's there just in case. Tell me you're not going to make me wear it now."

She gave him a considering look, then grinned. "Not now, but don't think you've escaped. Do you want to get out the tools for your makeover while I check the rest of your closet to see if there're any more surprises lurking?"

"There aren't, but have at it."

He headed into his bathroom, getting out some hair-friendly scissors as well as shaving gear. Jenny came in shortly thereafter, picking up the blades to inspect them. She snipped them together experimentally and laughed like a lunatic.

"If you think I'm going *GQ*," he said, "you're mistaken. And maybe I'm mistaken by letting you even get near me with those."

"It's just a trim, Liam. And don't look so nervous— I take care of my own hair at home."

He saw that she'd already immersed herself in this activity but, for some reason, it seemed as if she wasn't so much out to forget something as she was to have fun with what was happening in the here and now.

Imagine that. Him, Liam McCree, doing a "couple thing" like allowing a woman to cut his hair and shave his face, just so he could cheer her up.

Just so he could show her, and himself, that he trusted her.

She draped a towel around his shoulders and brought him to the bathtub, where he sat on the edge and hoped for the best. With the first metallic snip of his hair, he raised his hand, slowing her down.

"How much are you taking off?"

"A half inch." She grinned. "Maybe a full one."

He held back a groan. He was going to come out of this looking like a newscaster, wasn't he?

But…trust. He would work on placing some in her and take it from there. First he'd let her reveal the man underneath the hair and goatee, then the one under the clothing….

As she continued snipping, with his hair falling on the towel and into the tub, he made himself relax. But that really wasn't easy when she was near enough for him to smell her skin.

Damn, it'd tasted so good last night. And now, with Jenny running her fingers through his hair and cutting with soft snips of the scissors, he felt light-headed, thin-skinned.

"How long have you had the goatee?" she asked, her voice humming over him.

"Ever since I moved to Placid Valley," he said. "But in a former incarnation, it was one of those Vandyke beards."

"Suitably devilish."

She guided him to turn his head, her fingers gentle.

"Come to think of it," he said, "I've had beards of different assortments for years now."

Just another cover, right? He'd never actually realized that.

After a few minutes, she poised the scissors in the air and assessed her work. Then she slipped the towel from his shoulders and brushed off his neck. Her touch sent tiny lightning bolts through him, especially when she smoothed back his hair.

"Tell me what you think," she said as he got up from the tub's edge to go to the mirror.

There, he saw a man who still had longish hair, all one length, a bit like a clean-cut gypsy without the shagginess.

"Hip yet professional," Jenny said, clearly pleased. "Very McCree and Associates."

He caught her gaze in the mirror, his flesh heating.

Her skin pinkened, and she put down the scissors. But then, as if she didn't know what else to do, she pulled at her sweater.

No, Liam thought. He wasn't going to let anything else intrude.

"Need a razor?" he asked, grabbing the old-fashioned Gillette that he used to keep his goatee neat.

She blew out a breath, smiled, then took the razor from him. He leaned back against the sink's counter to close the height distance between them. He could tell that he'd lost a little bit of Jenny to her anxiety about the coming days, but he was going to get her back.

After turning on the faucet to fill the sink partway, she wet a washcloth, dampened his face with it, then squirted some lime shaving cream on her hand.

She slathered the foam over his chin, and with her this close again—near enough for him to see the flecks of silver in her blue eyes—he just about slipped his arms around her and pulled her to him.

But if Jenny wanted him, she only had to tell him.

He heard her swallow, heard her breathe, as she carefully placed her fingers on his cheek, positioning his face so she could shave him. That patch of skin burned, even when she relocated her fingers to his chin for leverage and carefully whisked the razor over the goatee.

They stayed like that, in silence, while she shaved him. And when she finally used the washcloth to remove the stubble and lather, the air hit his freshly uncovered skin, making it feel so much more tender, exposed, than it had before.

She brushed her fingertips over him there and, even with this new vulnerability, he didn't miss what he'd lost at all.

He had Jenny.

She no doubt saw the intensity in his gaze, because when she asked, "Do you want to see the results?" her tone was husky.

"Sure," he said, his own voice hardly more than a croak.

She cleared her throat and moved away from him as he turned to face the mirror.

Although he didn't do a double take, a moment passed before Liam really saw what was there—a guy who resembled the one in the college pictures he'd buried in a box in his parents' attic long ago.

But this mirrored image didn't have the same pre-accident innocence.

"You're ready to do business," Jenny said. "But you know what?"

He looked at her standing by his side in the mirror, and immediately, life improved.

"What?" he asked.

"I'm a fan of the way you were before," she said. "Not that this is bad. Heck, no. But…well, I kind of already miss the old Liam."

The man he'd made himself into.

Maybe there was room for a consolidation—old and new.

"I could always try the beard again," he said, rubbing his face, getting used to this bare look for the time being.

"Any way you come is fine with me," she said quietly.

Even in the reflection of the looking glass, he could see that she meant more than a haircut.

Although Jenny and Liam had gone to separate beds that night—maybe because he'd been waiting for her to make a move and she'd never done so—they decided to hang out the next day. So once again, she found herself at his place, where they worked together on more business plans while, this time, watching NFL football.

The interaction fulfilled Jenny, just as her job had done, but when she went home at the end of this day, too, she wasn't sure what to do with herself.

She couldn't work all the time; she wasn't even sure she wanted to. But what she did know for sure was that she hungered to still be with him.

Even so, as the hours counted down to her appointment, she told herself to be her own person, to depend on herself to get through life until her tissue sample was taken and her pathology report came in. Then…

Well, she wasn't going to dwell on it, she thought as she made her way down the street to the Suds Club early Monday afternoon. Mei greeted her at the door, just as if she'd been waiting for her.

Right after greeting her friend, Jenny automatically started scanning the room for Liam, forgetting for a moment that he'd said he would be here a little late today after a phone call with one of his college friends—a possible consultant.

Mei noticed.

"He's not here yet," she said.

"Oh."

Jenny was casual, but that was because she hadn't told Mei about getting together with Liam yet. Strange, because Jenny normally caught up with Mei after all her romantic adventures. But this time, it was almost as if Jenny might tarnish the memory once it hit the open air and she gave her friend the details.

Since the other women of the Club were at a folding table with their backs to the door, gathered around while Evina told a story about her last date, they'd said hey to Jenny and then gone back to listening.

Yet Mei's attention was all on her.

And why not? Jenny had already told Mei that Liam was able to take her to the appointment the day after tomorrow—oh man, the day after tomorrow—and it was obvious that something more than a kiss was going on between her and the corner businessman. It was just that Jenny had never left Mei out of the loop before.

She started to feel lost again—confused about who she was becoming—when the bell on the door sounded and Liam walked in and then over to her, carrying a cardboard tray with coffee and tea for them.

Maybe it was the lack of the goatee, his trimmed hair, his neater clothes or the absence of his computer, but no one seemed to recognize him at first.

Not until Vivian, the bike-short-wearing housewife, gave a delighted cry. "Talk about shining up!"

The rest of the women turned around from the folding table, then began aiming compliments and questions at him, and Liam looked ready to do an about-face and walk right back out the door.

Without thinking, Jenny grabbed his button-down, which he'd tucked into his jeans. Shrugging in acceptance, he grinned at her, and under the sway of him, she grinned back.

That was when the rest of the place went quiet.

Oops.

Suddenly, what she'd told Liam about becoming the Suds Club's own personal soap opera came to vivid reality as she recognized a glow of interest from the women.

Especially from Mei.

Her friend glanced at Liam's new look, then at Jenny. Then she smiled, practically giddy.

"I knew it," she whispered so no one else would hear.

Then, avoiding a scene, she gave them a discreet thumbs-up and turned around to take a seat for the soap opera, keeping their secret.

But Jenny was tired of secrets isolating her, tired of hanging on the outskirts of the group when she'd been so much a part of it before. She was tired of thinking she had no control over the direction her life was taking.

Impulse seized her, just as it had been doing so much lately, and she nestled her hand into Liam's free one, taking back the control while showing him that she was proud to be with him. That he was too good to be kept a secret.

They walked together to the seats, Liam raising an eyebrow at her as the Club *woo-woo*ed at them. Then they sat, waving the others off.

"And here I thought you were going to keep your scandalous association with me under cover," he said.

"I've got to stake my territory."

My God, she'd gone and said it, and now that the words were out, she realized how much she wanted them to be true. She didn't want him to go back to any other women. She wanted to shave him after they woke up together every morning, wanted to build a business with him.

But would life let her do that?

Would *she?*

She faced him, glad that there wasn't a seat between them this time, glad to see him sitting right here next to her even after all the trials she'd put him through.

"Once, you mentioned that you'd be lucky to have me," she said. "But I think I'm actually the luckiest one on earth."

He touched the back of her head, his gaze darkening with an intensity that she was getting to know all too well.

She answered him with an equally intense look that promised they were going to move further forward from this point on.

* * *

Liam and Jenny parted after their grand appearance at the Suds Club, but only because he had promised to cover the music store that Carl, one of his basketball pals, owned while the man suffered through a surprise home visit from his in-laws. After closing time, Liam and Jenny planned to go to a movie—hopefully something with a lot of loud noise that would block out the cacophony of his libido.

And after that?

They'd see, Liam guessed.

Just as he was flipping the sign on the door from OPEN to CLOSED, Jenny walked up to the mom-and-pop-type shop.

"Hey," he said, his voice giving every indication of just how glad he was to see her.

"Hi, there."

She beamed at him and came inside, and he noticed that she seemed relaxed in her jeans and a light blue sweater that was a little less huge than usual.

Could that be significant in some way?

Yet when she tugged at the edges of the cable knit, it was enough to hint that nothing had changed: she was as anxious about the upcoming appointment as ever, and he couldn't blame her.

While she wandered farther into the store, he secured the door, then took the cash drawer out of the register and made his way to the back office, where he would lock the money in the safe as he'd done when closing the store on a couple of other nights for Carl. But on the way back there, he stopped by Jenny, who was inspecting the pine bins holding the LPs. Back here, away from the CDs and DVDs positioned near the front, it smelled of musty wood and cardboard from the album covers, and more than even his apartment, it felt like home.

"This is neat," she said, scanning the displays and listening stations scattered around the area. "I've never been in here, even though I've lived in Placid Valley for years."

"This is what you find when you wander around a town."

Jenny thumbed through the plastic-sheathed covers. "Did you ever think that if you sold off some of the record collection you already have, you'd be able to rent a real office?"

He could tell she was kidding. Good. The more kidding, the better for her.

"No way I'm selling off anything," he said. "Consultants like me can work from home and visit the sites of my clients. Besides, I'd rather sell off stocks than my albums."

She nudged him with her hip. "Speaking of your collection, I've been—"

"—wondering…"

She laughed while continuing. "…why you're such a collector of those albums, anyway. They're records. They don't have nearly the sound quality of a CD."

"And CDs don't have half the personality of vinyl."

He flipped through a bin and held up a tattered copy of *Sergeant Pepper's Lonely Hearts Club Band.*

"This is art," he said, slipping the cover out of the plastic, "and it has real style with this gatefold cover—" he opened it up "—and cutout inserts." He put it back.

"My much older cousins had albums, and whenever I'd visit, I'd think they were so cool. The guys gave me an appreciation for them."

"Records remind you of family, then," she said.

He'd never thought of it that way before. "Well, I suppose so."

"You miss them?" Jenny asked. "Your family?"

"Yeah." He filed the Beatles album away. "I butted heads with my parents, as I mentioned before, but I do miss the gatherings, the unconditional love. I guess Placid Valley makes me think of home sometimes, though. It's the best of both worlds—a small town outside a bigger one."

"And you've got family here."

She put her hand on his waist, and he could see the longing in her gaze. But then she removed her hand, as if she was second-guessing herself.

Patience, he told himself.

He walked back to the office, and she followed.

"I think you know that *family* is hardly a term that applies to us," he said, setting the cash drawer on a desk. "But God help me, things are shifting around so fast between you and me that I don't know what to think anymore."

She leaned against a file cabinet. "I've wanted another night like the one we had before, Liam."

Fantasy churned through him: vivid memories of being against her, being inside her.

She continued. "But being with you once was something we could both work with, I think. Twice means something much more complicated."

"And you don't need complications."

"Probably not. But deep down, I do want them. With you."

Her eyes were wide, filled with fear, but also with desire.

Liam's blood raced until he had to exhale to relieve the ecstatic pressure.

She wanted him, but…

God, he would need to take the next step if he intended to have her in his future. Was he truly ready to reveal all of himself—even the scars?

"Jenny," he said, "is this is a good time? You've got a real trying day coming up."

"Yes, but I've gone over and over every reason to back off of intimacy. I've also thought of a million reasons why I want to be with you again…and again. And when it comes down to it, those reasons have everything to do with how I feel about *you* and not how I've been feeling about myself."

"But that last part's important," he said. "I need to know for certain that going forward will be the right thing for you to do."

"And the right thing for you, too." She cocked her head. "It didn't escape my attention that you didn't want to show those scars to me the other night."

He looked at her. Jenny, his ideal.

The woman he loved more than anything.

"All right," he said. "Then when you're ready, you just say the word."

She closed her eyes, then opened them to reveal such emotion that he fisted his hands.

"I want to be with you again, Liam."

His body went on high gear, everything heating up.

Yes.

She'd said yes.

But…

He was about to take the risk of seeing his own damaged self reflected back at him in her eyes.

And what if he saw that tiny jag of disgust splitting Jenny's gaze, just as he'd seen it in the past with another woman who'd broken him? What would he do then?

His heartbeat wavered as Jenny walked over to stroke his face. Then she kissed him, and the moment her lips touched his, the shields dropped away.

Leaving Liam as good as bare to her already.

Chapter Eleven

As Jenny kissed him, her pulse twanged her veins.

We have to trust each other. All the way.

But did she trust him? Or did she just *want* to?

Liam disengaged from their kiss and instead pressed his lips to her temple, her cheek, her lips again, as if wishing to cover all of her.

And uncover her, too.

Carried away by her need for him, she dug her fingers in his hair and pressed her mouth against his. They drew at each other, lost in a gale of passion, with her thinking, *My perfect man. My guy.*

But who was she to him? Friend and lover? Or was there another element that had been growing in the back of her mind—another excuse to avoid true intimacy? A feeling that he was a damaged person, just like she might be.

The word shot through her. *Damaged*.

Was she?

Denying it, fighting it with every thrashing cell of her being, she kissed him harder, until they both had to come up for breath. Then she rested her hands on his chest, burying her face in the crook of his neck as they recovered.

She grasped at what she knew, what made her comfortable.

"Even the first time I saw you," she said, her mouth brushing his skin, "you captured my interest. You were sitting in a chair, reading a magazine, waiting for your wash. You didn't have your computer."

"I was scoping the place out," he said, running his hands up her back, over her sweater.

Then he stopped at the bottom of it, sliding his fingers beneath the knit.

Her heart jackhammered at her breastbone.

"I thought you might be a little arrogant," she said, "because your back was halfway to the room, like you didn't want anyone to approach." In spite of her determination to stay in control, she skimmed her hands over his chest, feeling the smooth ridges of muscle. A tremor lined the inside of her belly, driving her to tug his shirt out of his pants, to softly kiss his neck.

He gripped her sweater. "But then I saw you, and I knew I was going to be back the next day."

"You didn't come back just for the office space?"

"God, no, Jenny. Haven't you figured that out by now?"

Her body, her head, went light and achy.

All that time, and she'd never realized…

So what did that say about her perception these days? Had her judgment improved at all?

The fear returned to her bloodstream—fear of failing. Fear of not knowing what to do or who to turn to if everything eventually fell apart.

But it wouldn't, she told herself.

It couldn't.

She slid her hand under Liam's cotton shirt, almost as if she needed reassurance, then pressed her palms just below his shoulder blades. His scent worked its way into her, deeper, lower, becoming such a part of her that she felt wound up in him, tangled.

Her inner guardian pinched her, as if in warning, but she wasn't sure why. It was only a niggle, a buried threat that she couldn't figure out yet.

Taking her hands out from under the material, she undid Liam's shirt, button by button. And when she was done, she peeled off the clothing.

His torso was something an artist would shape out of marble: ridged abs, smooth bumps of muscle over ribs, the firmness of a broad chest, the sturdiness of arms that took frequent part in physical activity. Her breathing went shallow, and she skimmed her fingertips over the line of downy hair that disappeared into his waistband.

He leaned back against the wall, his hands clenching her waist and bringing her with him.

When she looked into his eyes, she recognized the wariness, and she knew it was from always keeping himself a few feet away from a crowd, always making sure that no one had the chance to injure him again.

But she wanted to show him that, in his clothes or out of them, he took her breath away.

"Back when I first saw you," she said, starting on the button at his fly, "I should've expected that you'd look this way underneath those shirts and jeans. You're the perfect one, Liam. The perfect man."

"Not so perfect." His voice was almost gravelly with the anticipation of how she was going to react when she got to his leg.

"You're perfect for me," she said.

She unzipped his fly, but it wasn't a sexual moment as much as purely emotional, with her easing down his pants. Then, without looking down, she pressed against him for another kiss. With her lips, she told him that she was going to accept everything about him.

She kissed his jaw, then traveled down to his neck, to his chest, his ribs, until she slid the rest of the way down, down to his knee.

A clock ticked somewhere in the room while she took in what he'd been keeping from her.

The scars.

They formed an intricate web of healed flesh above and below his knee, and she pressed her fingertips to his skin, pressed her lips there, too.

Then she grabbed Liam's hand and pulled him down to the floor to be with her.

As he sat against the wall and met her gaze, Jenny kept her fingers on his injury.

She didn't have to say anything, because she was sure he could see that she was thinking those scars were marks of experience and growth, just like the ones everyone carried somewhere to some extent, whether on the inside or out.

That they were a beautiful part of him, an integral component that told her where he'd been and what he'd overcome.

As she bent to rest her cheek against his knee, she could see the sublime relief in his own gaze, and it filled her with such joy that she didn't know how to respond.

But the inner guardian that hounded her seemed to know what to say.

You should get out of here now, it whispered. *You've come to depend on him. You've come to need him* too *much.*

The thought was shocking in its brutal truth.

She fought off the warnings, even if she knew they were only trying to protect her.

In the meantime, Liam had reached out, resting his fingers under her chin. She smiled, wanting so badly to keep him happy. So badly to keep this going.

"How could I look at you any differently when I already knew what you were made of?" she asked.

"Jenny…"

Her name said it all: his happiness at having found her, his great fortune at having someone who accepted him body and soul.

To her, it'd never been a question of how she was going to react. Yet would he return the sentiment if it came time for her to show *him* any damage?

Liam gathered Jenny close, pulling her onto his lap to bury his face in her hair. He sketched his hand down her back, then up, memorizing and absorbing.

He was still reeling from what he'd seen in her—a woman who recognized the best in him—and he longed to show her that he could be the same pillar for her. That he would always see to the heart of Jenny, too.

Without rushing it, he began to ease her sweater off her shoulder. She took hold of his wrist. Frustration ate through him, but only because he thought they'd gotten beyond this. But he realized now that there was still a part of her that required care and patience.

"What do you think will happen if that sweater comes off?" Liam asked softly.

She paused, and even though he sensed that something had changed from the moment she'd seen his leg until now, he forged ahead in his desire to keep her with him.

"Like you said," he murmured, "how could I look at you differently when I already know what you're made of?"

She sat up, her gaze reflecting a growing confusion that he'd seen before and had tried to fight.

"Maybe it's just going to take more time," she said. *More time.* It sounded like a gentle excuse.

Didn't she know that he could guarantee she had nothing to worry about when it came to him? Or was she trying to control this small detail when the rest of the world was spinning off its axis around her?

"Okay, Jenny," he said. His tone betrayed disappointment at the slam of her not believing in him. But he would keep on believing in her, no matter how hard it got.

"You're hurt," she said, pulling her sweater back onto her shoulder.

"I love you too much to be that petty," he said.

His confession left the same look in her eyes that he'd

expected to find when she'd seen his scars, not when he'd told her that he loved her.

His chest seemed to fall into the hole his heart had just left.

He released her, allowing her to go if she wished to.

But she stayed on his lap, even though she felt farther away than ever.

"I said it too soon," he said.

"Liam, being with you is one thing, but right now love is…"

"A complication," he finished.

She shook her head. "I don't know what it is. I don't know if what I'm feeling for you is love or if it's need or—"

"A gravitational pull between one wounded person and another."

She widened her eyes, and he could tell that the thought had crossed her mind.

Ouch.

He eased her off his lap, then started to put his clothing—and himself—back together.

"You can admit it," he said. "You think I overheard the news about your lump, and that made me think that you were the only kind of person I could ever feel good around. But you haven't been listening to me."

"Liam—"

"No." He held up a finger. "Listen now, because I'm here to tell you that I've carried my love for you around for about a year now, and it has everything to do with how you make a room light up when you walk into it and how you make me feel when you do even a little thing like smile."

Jenny seemed to be battling—he could see it on her face. But she was trying too hard to keep herself emotionally unavailable, and maybe she would always be from this point on.

"You make me feel like I used to when I ran," he said. "Free. High on everything around me."

"It doesn't scare you to have someone make you feel like that?" she asked in a small voice. "Haven't you ever thought that maybe you should be able to make yourself feel that way without having to depend on someone else?"

"No, because loving you doesn't make me weaker." As she watched, he paused in buttoning his shirt. "These past days, loving you has built me up to a point where I never wanted to come down."

Jenny gathered the sweater around her. "But I do bring you down. You see that, right? And it's not fair to you. It hurts to see what I'm doing to you even now."

He opened his mouth to answer, then stopped, his eyes haunted by an anguished darkness that swallowed her, too.

Jenny held back a terrible, ripping sadness. See—she was the one who made him uncertain about what to say. It was passion for each other that had brought him up, but it was reality that would smack him to the floor every time.

She wasn't good for anyone right now, least of all Liam.

Why had she thought any differently?

She knew the truth: because she'd been selfish.

She'd wanted him all to herself in a greedy, blissful rush that had made her forget what was looming ahead of her.

And if there was one thing she knew, it was that love wasn't selfish. Love didn't and shouldn't bring agony to the other person. Love was about letting someone go when you knew that all you were going to do was make their life worse.

Jenny rose to her feet, her knees wobbly. Before she lost her balance, she held on to the desk.

But Liam wasn't done with her.

"Don't you walk out that door," he said.

He was on his feet now, and his physical presence was enough to make her entire body slant toward him of its own accord.

His determined expression tore the heart out of her.

"No matter what you say," he whispered urgently, "I'm always going to love you. And I'm never going to stop, even if you push me away."

Tears gathered in her eyes, blurring her vision. "Liam, you're the best thing that's ever happened to me, but I just can't do this anymore." Do this to him. "I can't."

Before she changed her mind, she turned around and went through the exit, closing the door behind her while she rushed away.

But as she left the store, she found it was much harder to close her heart.

Jenny hardly slept that night, mostly because of the regret making her stare at the walls.

Mostly because she kept seeing the undying affection and determination on Liam's face when she'd left him.

That inner guardian tried to soothe her.

You made the right decision, it said. *You'll be able to depend on yourself to get through this. You didn't need him.*

Oh, but she did, and it didn't have to do with requiring a shoulder to lean on as much as with enjoying every moment she'd spent with him. Living life to its fullest with him by her side.

Would it be such a bad thing to allow him to take a little of the weight off her shoulders? Couldn't she still be the independent Jenny who was trying so hard to get through all of this?

She rose early, wandering through her apartment in search of something to keep her occupied. Meanwhile, she reminded herself that she would have to ask Mei to drive her to the appointment tomorrow. Or maybe she could just call a taxi.

Brave Jenny could manage that.

When she sauntered past the second bedroom, which she used as a well-organized office, she caught a glimpse of the papers on the desk.

Some sketches and notes for Liam's business.

Anguish pushed down on her, and she continued back to her room, where she decided to shower and get ready. Then she would call Mei, since her friend would already be up with her daughter while Travis was on shift at the firehouse.

An hour and a half later, she was sitting at Mei's kitchen table, thankful to have someplace to be while the clock ticked, ticked.

Guessing at Jenny's anxiety, Mei had devised a project that young Isabel could also participate in—putting together a scrapbook of "happy pictures," as the little girl called them.

And the ruse was working for the time being, as Jenny looked over a photo that featured Isabel at her first birthday party.

"That's me!" The girl was sitting next to Jenny, her dark hair in braids, her miniature body dressed in a ruffled pink top and pants. "Were you at my party, Jen?"

"Yes, I was." She took in the festive hats, the smiles, the creamy cake with one candle on it. "I'd just met your mom at the Club shortly before this, but we were good friends right off the bat."

Across the table, Mei was writing checks for the household bills, and she glanced up, smiling. "Jenny had just settled into her apartment."

Isabel crawled onto Jenny's lap to get a better look at the picture, and Jenny held the little girl, wrapping her arms around her. A lump formed in her throat as she wondered what her and Liam's children might have looked like one day, if she ever got the chance to have them.

Would they have dark hair or light hair? Would they be lean like him or have curves like her? Would they have his devilish smile?

At the memory of his face, pain stabbed her chest, but she went on to the next picture in order to erase him—and the decision she'd made—from her mind.

Still, her throat stung even more.

She held a photo of herself dressed in a parachute-jumping suit, her thumbs up.

"Why do you look so funny?" Isabel asked.

Mei answered. "Because Jenny decided she wanted to fling herself out of a plane while Mommy stayed safely on the ground and took pictures."

"Your mom came close to doing it," Jenny said to the little girl.

"But I was a chicken." Mei laughed and scribbled out another check.

"Was it scary to jump?" Isabel asked.

"Yes." Jenny's throat closed even more, because hopping out of that plane had made her stomach clench, but it was nothing next to real life.

Nothing next to what she felt every time she thought about what she'd done to Liam.

"But," she added, fighting to keep her ground, her sanity, "jumping was exhilarating, too. I got to fly."

Isabel threw an arm around Jenny's neck.

"Oh, I want to fly!"

They all did, Jenny thought, and she'd had her chance with Liam, only to fall. The irony was that she'd been afraid of falling or failing her whole life, and every time she had, things hadn't turned out so badly.

Take her job, for instance. When she'd gotten laid off, it hadn't crushed her at all.

Not like leaving the man she loved last night…

Love. The word chopped at her. It had so many angles, and she was starting to wonder if she'd only been concentrating on the wrong ones—the ones that had protected her and provided her with excuses to leave him before he left her.

If she loved Liam, wouldn't she refuse to shut him out like this?

Isabel snuggled against her, and Jenny could tell that the girl had lost some energy. Mei winked at Jenny.

She held Isabel tighter. It felt good, and she didn't even feel weaker for using her as comfort. But that particular realization kicked in the most devastating truth of all.

Love wasn't a destroyer—it was a uniter, and it could piece a person back together when she'd started to come apart.

As Jenny kept sorting through the pictures with one hand, she eventually felt Isabel's breathing even out. She hugged the girl to her.

A husband, children, a life.

Why *couldn't* she have them all?

Why should she be stopped from taking every moment as it came, just like Liam's uncle Tommy, and tackling each happy accident or daunting challenge? Why should she be stopped from being the absolute happiest she could be?

Jenny rose from her chair to put Isabel in her bedroom, determination racing through her. When her inner guardian started up again, she shut it down.

For good this time.

After tucking Isabel in, she went back to the table, where Mei was cleaning up.

"I need to go to Liam," Jenny said, nearly breathless by now.

Her friend smiled. "I was hoping you'd say that."

* * *

Liam hadn't even bothered to go into the Suds Club today. It didn't seem like a need-to-be-here place now, based on what had happened with Jenny last night.

He could wait for her to walk through the door all he wanted, but it wouldn't be the same. Instead of his pulse jumping with anticipation every time the entrance bell dinged, his heart would instead die a little when he saw someone else.

He would know that Jenny had pushed him away for what might be the last time.

So Liam told himself to stay put, sitting at his messy desk at home and going through his papers. Demons kept screeching at him, mocking him with the possibility that she'd just hidden her contempt for his scars really well and that this was truly the reason she'd left. But he couldn't quite bring himself to believe that, not after he'd seen what he'd thought was returned love in her gaze.

And heard it in her last words to him.

Even though you're the best thing that's ever happened to me...

That had to mean something, right?

He looked at all the papers before him, then got to his feet and grabbed his wallet.

Damn it, he couldn't sit around cooped up in his studio anymore. Not when Jenny was out there somewhere.

While he walked down the street, he had no plan, he had no grand scheme. He just had hope, which was, admittedly, running in short supply. But it was there all the same.

He entered the Club to find the usual crowd, yet they were so intent upon chatting with a new woman that they didn't even notice his entrance.

After a visual sweep, he saw that Jenny wasn't there. His stomach felt as if a bar of lead had settled at the bottom of it. Maybe, in an attempt to avoid him, she would never come here again.

The weight got heavier as he leaned against the dryers, his heart just as leaden now. Yet then the bell on the door dinged, and he looked over to find her at the entrance, her breath short, as if she'd been running.

He stood, pushed up by the explosion in his chest.

She didn't move for a moment—long enough for him to see that her heart was in her eyes. Then, as she came forward, his own heart put itself back together and then expanded, filling him until it threatened to take him over.

But he allowed it. He welcomed it.

A few feet away, she halted, her lips parted.

"Jenny?" he asked, all his hopes laid bare for her to take or leave.

Then her mouth broke into a smile that had the potential to brighten all the days ahead of them.

"I came here to finally tell you," she said as the rest of the room went quiet, "that I love you more than anyone or anything I've ever loved before, Liam McCree."

Chapter Twelve

Jenny had confessed her love loud and clear, for all the room to hear. For all the world, as far as she was concerned. She didn't care who knew how she felt—she was finished being the woman who was too proud to share her woes, the woman who didn't reach out for whatever or whoever she needed.

Jenny fisted her hands, holding on to hope this time.

Just pure hope and nothing more.

As Liam stood in front of those dryers, he seemed at a loss for words and, for a ridiculous moment, hope slipped from Jenny's grasp.

He couldn't have changed his mind so soon, she thought. Not Liam, the man who'd proclaimed his love just last night.

Then he stepped forward and took her in his arms, bringing her against him in a crush of fervid acceptance.

Every cell within Jenny smacked together and caused a quaking explosion, and when he spoke, he tickled her ear with his words.

"I love you, too, Jenny. I love you so damned much."

Seemingly a universe away, she barely heard the members of the Suds Club break into applause. But the sound was muffled because her head was filled with *him*.

Her Liam.

Her future.

"You ran over here to tell me?" he added, while in the background, the Club's applause gave way to a rapt silence.

She nodded against his chest, her cheek scratching his shirt.

"I went to your place first, then realized you were probably here," she said. "But I would've gone miles at full speed to tell you. I didn't want to continue even one more minute without being honest about what I'm feeling, no matter what happens after this."

Liam tilted her chin up so she could meet that constant gaze of his.

He could obviously sense the worry that was still eating at her, but as always, he understood. And she knew that Liam would be at her side every step of the way while they figured out how to live every day from here on out.

He bent to kiss her, and she made a small sound of anticipation. His lips gently touched hers.

The members of the Club *awww*ed.

Both Jenny and Liam pulled back and looked at the crowd, who were clasping their hands to their chests while they tilted their heads in appreciation of a happy scene. Domestic goddess Vivian was even dabbing at her eyes as she stood next to a woman Jenny had never seen before.

A new member?

"Like we told you," the housewife said to the initiate. "This place is magic."

Next to Vivian, Evina pulled a tissue from her purse, her eyes bright. "We can call Naomi and Dave in New York and invite them to the wedding!"

Suddenly Jenny couldn't breathe at the return to reality.

A wedding.

She glanced at Liam to find that he hadn't been shocked by the idea at all. But he *couldn't* have thought that far into the future.

Or had he been way ahead of her again?

He guided her toward the door. "Time for us to talk," he said.

"Big time for us to talk," she added.

They said goodbye to the group, which was already aflutter with plans for a bride-and-groom shower, and went outside.

Once they were on the sidewalk, Liam took her by the hand and led her in the direction of his apartment. As they crossed the street, Jenny was finally able to brush the shock out of her mind and wrangle a good breath. But she couldn't stop her blood from whizzing around her heart as they passed his complex's entrance gate, then came to his apartment.

"They've got it all planned out for us, don't they?" Jenny asked while he unlocked his door.

Her voice trembled a little.

"You told me you loved me," he said, giving her his full attention, as always, "but it sounds like you're still afraid. Are you?"

She gave a slight nod, feeling as if she'd jumped into a car and it had peeled out to take the sharp curves of a road before she'd had the opportunity to buckle herself in.

Yet she was *always* buckling herself in, even long before she needed to. Wasn't that the reason she'd shrugged off her defenses and run to Liam to tell him how she felt? Because she was tired of being held down?

He stroked her cheek with his knuckles, and it was as if he had transferred a current of optimism into her.

"Don't be afraid, Jenny," he said.

She couldn't help believing in him, because with him by her side, his hand over hers, she could hold on.

They could.

Gazing up at him—at that clean-shaven face with its gorgeous angles and everlasting trust—Jenny grabbed his shirt.

Holding.

"Lately," she said, "I've been doing things I normally wouldn't do, mainly out of fear. And I was so busy searching for fast answers that I overlooked what was right in front of me."

"But you see me now."

"And I'll never stop seeing you." She pulled him closer, drowning in the pools of his light-brown eyes, the promise of his devotion. "Your love has gone hand in hand with happiness, and it took a while for me to understand that. Through you, I finally found myself."

"The stalwart, funny, smart woman I've always loved. Thing is, I always knew she was there."

He ran his fingers over her hair, and she closed her eyes, craving for him to make her all his.

"You can be anything you want to be," he added. "Outstanding businesswoman, best friend…" His voice took on a strained, yearning note. "Lover."

Her eyes opened on that last part, and she saw that he would climb mountains to make all of it come true.

"I want to be more than just those things someday." Emotion dug its claws into her. "I want to be a mother, Liam, and I've really never realized that until recently. Work seemed to fulfill a lot of needs, but then you made me realize that it wasn't enough."

If she'd expected him to back away, like other men might have, he didn't.

Instead, his eyes took on a joyful glow. "Having a family with you would be more than I'd ever believed I could have."

Real life crept in again, darkening her a little.

But what if I can't manage a family? she wondered. What if, what if, what if…?

He cupped her face in his hands.

"You can be anything," he reminded her.

Affection, pure belief—they welled up and overtook her.

"Even," he said, "a wife."

The statement floated between them for a moment—

so nebulous that she could almost reach through it. But then, as he smiled, she could see their future, and she took it by grasping his hand.

"Marry me, Jenny Hunter," he said, his voice catching on her name. "Be my wife along with everything else you already are."

Even back when Liam had first fallen for Jenny, he hadn't been completely reconciled to the idea of getting married, mostly because he hadn't thought that a woman would ever have him.

Especially her.

But now, with her cheeks flushed and her blue eyes shining, Liam could see himself in a tux at the front of a church, a man who was together and whole because of the woman who'd convinced him that he could be no other way.

In her tear-sparkled eyes, he saw himself taking vows he meant with every last part of his soul, and he saw her, too, in a glamorous wedding dress that kissed her curves. A dress that made her all woman, no matter what she might soon have to physically endure.

She raised her face to him, tears on her cheeks.

Jenny. So amazing, so absolutely necessary to the rest of his life.

"Yes," she said. "Yes, I'll marry you."

Bliss roared through him, and he laughed, so damned emotional that he crushed her against him in an embrace that told her how sunny their days would be together. He led her mouth to his, and at first, they were tender with each other, sweet, as he kissed the salt of her tears away from the corners of her lips. But then passion got hold of him—uncontrollable and fiery—and when he fully kissed her, her mouth parted under his.

He slid his tongue into her, exploring with humid strokes, and she pulled on his shirt, bringing him closer, closer, until his heated groin was flush against her belly.

"I think we need to go inside," she whispered.

"Yeah."

He opened the door, but before they entered, he picked her up by the waist and lifted her.

On a gasp, she braced her hands on his shoulders, and they both laughed.

Yet the moment turned serious as he lowered her, allowing her to slide down his body, inch by agonizing inch, until they were face-to-face.

Wrapping his arms around her to keep her lips just a whisper away from his, he carried her over his threshold, then set her on her feet.

"Marriage," she said, as if just now realizing what it truly meant.

"Are you thinking of how long our savings will last?" he asked as he closed the door behind them. "Because there're practical matters, to be sure."

"It doesn't change anything," she said. "I told you that I've got a lot saved up, probably even enough to get us through the lean years of the business."

"Which you'll be a partner in?"

She smiled. "I'll be a partner in everything."

With restrained need, he kissed her softly once again, then spoke against her mouth.

"Good," he said. "And you should know that when

I told you I had stocks last night, I meant that I had stocks."

She backed away, furrowing her brow. Then her face registered understanding.

"A decent businessman," he said, "always puts aside something for the future."

"Liam McCree."

She laughed softly, and the vibration of it traveled through his skin.

"I told you before," she said, "there are more than just jeans in your closet."

One arm still around her, he gestured toward his shelves of LPs. "I also have more than a few rare albums locked away, so no worries on the monetary front."

At her amazed look, he shrugged, then kissed her again, and the air around them seemed to swelter, enveloping them. His body all but melted into the atmosphere, into her, and when her hand crept between them, it jarred him out of his haze. But she wasn't pushing him away or providing a barrier this time.

She was starting to unbutton her sweater.

His breathing was short as he asked, "Are you sure?"

"I've never been so sure of anything."

Their look was long, drawn out by how much he wanted all of her.

"Pull out the futon?" she asked, undoing another button.

He kissed her, lingering, then went to do her bidding, his pulse stamping out every second until he was barley able to think.

Jenny was uncovering the rest of herself because she loved him.

This is really happening, he thought. *And it's not just for a night.*

By the time he had the futon pulled out and ready, she'd parted the front of her sweater to reveal a baggy gray T-shirt underneath. She'd removed her shoes, too, and he took the opportunity to do the same.

His body's vitals skyrocketed as she came to stand before him in what seemed to be an invitation for him to take off her sweater.

It was a gesture that would mean so much more than merely stripping down for a lovemaking session.

It was the first step to truly moving on.

He inhaled deeply, sliding the sweater down her shoulders, then her arms, until it was off and crumpled on the floor.

They were so close, so attuned, that he thought he could feel her pounding heartbeat inside his own chest, as if they were already joined.

Then she began to lift her T-shirt over her head, and he helped her, then discarded that, too.

And there she stood in her pretty dark blue lace bra and jeans, her curves so beautiful that they made him throb all over.

He touched her waist, his thumb trailing over her belly. The muscles there jerked while he rubbed back and forth over her velvety skin. Then she unbuttoned the fly of her jeans and made her way out of them.

He took off his own shirt. But before he did away with his trousers, she reached out to him, then brought him to the futon. She sat on the edge of it, looking a little unsure, even after all they'd said to each other.

He gave her a smile, and that put one back on her face, too. Then she lay back on the mattress, opening her arms to him.

Blood thundered as he poised himself above her, then kissed her. Afterward, he reclined on his side and leisurely stroked a hand down one of her arms and back up again.

"You're so damned soft," he said.

He transferred his attention to her stomach, tracing his fingers over it.

She laughed, obviously tickled, and he dragged his fingers down to her belly.

There, he sketched around and around as her muscles reacted.

"You're driving me crazy," she said.

"We've got all the time in the world for that." He bent down to kiss her belly button, to ring it with his tongue.

Her skin carried a hint of honey today, and he pictured her in the shower, slathering gel over her skin, then afterward, smoothing lotion up and down and around.

He got hard even fantasizing about it, and that inspired him.

"Don't move," he said, rolling off the futon, then raising a finger to indicate he'd be right back.

And he was, within seconds, after he grabbed a bottle of lotion from his bathroom.

He crawled back onto the mattress with it.

"I thought you said I was soft," she murmured as he dispensed some lotion onto his palm and rubbed his hands together.

"You are soft." He smiled wickedly. "But I had a

fantasy, and there was something about massaging you all over that got to me."

Besides, he thought, he wanted to do everything he could to relax her.

He smoothed his hands over her belly and upward, and the slick contact was sensuous, languid, causing her to close her eyes and raise her hands over her head.

There, he thought, using his thumbs to apply pressure to her upper stomach.

She arched beneath his firm touch, making a contented sound, and he massaged his way over to her arms, then her shoulders.

He was working his way to her breasts, hesitant about whether it was too soon. She had opened her eyes, and the second his gaze connected with hers, a volt of longing charged him.

This craving he saw reflected in her… Damn, it was almost too much for him to handle.

She reached to the front of her bra to unhook it, and the area around his heart pushed inward, as if threatening to make him pop altogether.

Then she opened her bra, revealing her breasts.

Liam looked into her eyes, and she took both his hands and led them to her.

Jenny wanted to feel Liam's hands on her, giving her pleasure and bringing her to the same peak that he'd brought her to the other night.

Her husband-to-be, she thought, willing to give everything over to him, because they were two people who'd already become one.

Two people who knew where they belonged.

As he touched the underside of her right breast, she sighed and raised her hands over her head again, letting him take over.

Trusting him implicitly.

He circled his thumbs over her nipples, slowly, then took both of her breasts in his palms, feeling every inch of them.

She held her breath.

"Open your eyes, Jenny."

She did, seeing in his own gaze that he would never judge her. That he would always want her for more than her body.

"I love you," he said, and it wasn't so much a reminder as much as something he enjoyed saying.

Emotion pierced her. "I love you, too."

When his mouth latched onto her right nipple, she shifted her hips, delight rising in her and blasting away every thought of what was happening outside of their own little world.

His tongue swirled, making her feel like there was a twister inside her that was gathering force and speed, spreading up and down her body and tearing apart everything in its path.

She was getting damp, her body priming itself for him as he sucked on her.

"Liam," she said, and she barely recognized the demand in her tone.

But when she sat up and pulled him to her so they could kiss some more—how she adored kissing him—

she knew he would love this insistent side of her, too, as he loved everything else about her.

She swept her tongue into his mouth, and they sucked and laved, establishing an escalating need and rhythm.

She groaned again and gently pushed him onto his back, shrugging off the rest of her bra, straddling him, then digging through his pockets for those condoms she knew he kept there.

Even though she ached to have his children someday, right now she wanted him all to herself.

She brought out two condoms and set them on the mattress.

"Come out and play?" she asked, feeling so free at knowing she could be anything—naughty minx, shy girl, devoted fiancée—that she could barely contain herself.

"Anytime," he said.

"I knew you'd say that."

She reached into his fly and brought him out. He was already stiff, and her body tightened at the sight of him.

Unable to bear it any longer, she rose to take off her panties, allowing him the room to work off his pants at the same time.

When she'd gotten her panties off, she came back down to him, then grabbed one condom while he got the other.

Then, working together, she slipped the rubber over his arousal, and he followed with the second layer.

Afterward, she bent over him, fitting her lips to his, breath to breath, as she positioned herself over his tip, pausing.

"Come on, Jenny," he said.

She smiled against his mouth and lowered herself

onto him, and his resulting groan shuddered into her: through her own mouth, down through her chest, spreading lower and hotter.

He held her hips as she began to gyrate, taking in as much of him as she could.

Leaning back her head, she kept her fingertips on his chest, where sweat was misting. Then, wanting to feel all of him, she lowered her body until she was flat against him, her breasts crushed to him.

With each churning motion of her hips, they slipped and slid, friction providing an inner heat that joined with the twister that had been stirring her up inside.

But now it was a column of fire, rising within her, burning and whirling.

Liam sat up, keeping them pasted to each other while allowing them to increase the pace, to drive and circle against each other, to go deeper.

As they labored, excitement joined the fire within her, lifting it even higher, widening it until the flames swallowed her body and mind with a soaring burn.

It crisped her, singed her, but she embraced the heat as it spun her, dizzied her, whipped her inside out until she thought it might consume her altogether.

But then she felt Liam entwining his fingers with hers, and she held on tight, higher, hotter, brighter…

As she burst into an inferno, she felt even stronger than before, a new being forged from this man, this love.

She helped him to come to completion, too, and when he finally thrust into her, crying out, she kept holding his hand until he floated down from his ecstatic heights.

Then he fell back to the mattress, taking her with him, and they stayed glued together, body to body, soul to soul.

They kissed each other again, connected and invincible, and Jenny knew that nothing could beat what they'd created between the two of them.

Nothing at all.

Epilogue

In a condo near Jasmine Trails Avenue that Liam and Jenny had purchased just last year, Liam sat in the second-bedroom office and read a forwarded e-mail from Mei.

"It's about Baby Boom-Boom," he said, referring to their friend's online baby-clothing business.

Jenny glanced up from her spot on the floor where she was organizing paperwork for one of the bigger companies who employed McCree & McCree as consultants. It was the middle of winter, and she was wearing a sweater, but it wasn't baggy.

It was a typical sweater that showed off her curves to every advantage.

She'd obviously sensed the excitement in his voice, but that didn't surprise him when they were so often of one mind.

He turned in his chair to face his wife. "Mei says that a major department store is interested in carrying her line."

"Are you kidding?"

Jenny sprang to her feet and came over to the computer to look over his shoulder while sliding her palm over his chest. The clover scent of her made his heart beat, just as if he'd come off of a long, cleansing run.

"Kidding?" he asked, pressing a kiss to the inside of her arm. "Who, me?"

She hugged him to herself as she read the e-mail, and his shoulder brushed her left breast.

It'd been a long, rough road since the day they'd gotten engaged. A biopsy had ended up yielding positive results for a tumor, and as Liam had promised, he'd been with her every minute during preparations for the lumpectomy and the radiation treatments.

It'd all resulted in a report of clear margins in her breast, which allowed them a great measure of relief, knowing that there were no cancerous cells in the tissue that had surrounded the tumor. They were still vigilant about watching for any return of the cancer, but that didn't stop them from living each day to the fullest.

They had nurtured their business, using his college friends as additional consultants, hiring on two more and even traveling to places like Italy and Ireland in the time they made to enjoy life and each other.

He'd met her parents when they'd come out after her diagnosis, but Liam and Jenny had traveled even more when he'd brought her back to Kansas to meet his family after they'd eloped.

As Liam had predicted, Uncle Tommy had wholeheartedly approved of Jenny. Hell, he'd even taken both her and Liam to the basement, away from everyone else at the family gathering, to fix them highballs.

Now, as Liam rubbed her arm, his wife finished reading Mei's e-mail and laughed, obviously happy for her friend. She kissed Liam's cheek, which was freshly shaven, since he hadn't ever grown back any kind of beard.

"I suppose we'll have to step up Mei's business planning," she said.

"Seems so." He eased her onto his lap. "She's going to have a lot to deal with."

"A little girl, an even younger boy, another pregnancy, and now a bigger business, too. But Travis is there for her. So are we."

"Are you up to the challenge of growing her business?" She gave him a sassy smile.

"I'm up for anything."

Then she leaned forward to put her mouth on his, kissing him senseless, those beautiful lips taking him to places far beyond anywhere he'd gone before.

After ending their long kiss with a sweet, shorter one, he slid his hand under her sweater.

"Are you even up for giving it a go tonight?" he asked.

"How about right now?"

They were just starting to try to get pregnant, having been told by the doctors that waiting a couple of years after her ordeal would be a good idea.

Liam cupped his hand over her belly, where he hoped their child would be growing soon, and such overwhelming love and gratefulness filled him that he had to swallow to keep from being utterly overwhelmed.

"I love you so much," Jenny said.

And that made his throat tighten even more, but not enough to keep his own fervent promise from rushing out.

"I love you, too, Jenny McCree."

They kissed again, eager to get started on growing their own family business.

* * * * *

Here's a sneak peek at
THE CEO'S CHRISTMAS PROPOSITION,
the first in USA TODAY *bestselling author*
Merline Lovelace's HOLIDAYS ABROAD *trilogy*
coming in November 2008.

American Devon McShay is about to get the Christmas surprise of a lifetime when she meets her new client, sexy billionaire Caleb Logan, for the very first time.

Silhouette
Desire

Available November 2008

Her breath whistled out in a sigh of relief when he exited Customs. Devon recognized him right away from the newspaper and magazine articles her friend and partner Sabrina had looked up during her frantic prep work.

Caleb John Logan, Jr. Thirty-one. Six-two. With jet-black hair, laser-blue eyes and a linebacker's shoulders under his charcoal-gray cashmere overcoat. His jaw-dropping good looks didn't score him any points with Devon. She'd learned the hard way not to trust handsome heartbreakers like Cal Logan.

But he was a client. An important one. And she was willing to give someone who'd served a hitch in the marines before earning a B.S. from the University of Oregon, an MBA from Stanford and his first million at the ripe old age of twenty-six the benefit of the doubt.

Right up until he spotted the hot-pink pashmina, that is.

Devon knew the flash of color was more visible than the sign she held up with his name on it. So she wasn't surprised when Logan picked her out of the crowd and cut in her direction. She'd just plastered on her best businesswoman smile when he whipped an arm around her waist. The next moment she was sprawled against his cashmere-covered chest.

"Hello, brown eyes."

Swooping down, he covered her mouth with his.

Sheer astonishment kept Devon rooted to the spot for a few seconds while her mind whirled chaotically. Her first thought was that her client had downed a few too many drinks during the long flight. Her second, that he'd mistaken the kind of escort and consulting services her company provided. Her third shoved everything else out of her head.

The man could kiss!

His mouth moved over hers with a skill that ignited sparks at a half dozen flash points throughout her body. Devon hadn't experienced that kind of spontaneous combustion in a while. A *long* while.

The sparks were still popping when she pushed off his chest, only now they fueled a flush of anger.

"Do you always greet women you don't know with a lip-lock, Mr. Logan?"

A smile crinkled the skin at the corners of his eyes. "As a matter of fact, I don't. That was from Don."

"Huh?"

"He said he owed you one from New Year's Eve two years ago and made me promise to deliver it."

She stared up at him in total incomprehension. Logan hooked a brow and attempted to prompt a non-existent memory.

"He abandoned you at the Waldorf. Five minutes before midnight. To deliver twins."

"I don't have a clue who or what you're..."

Understanding burst like a water balloon.

"Wait a sec. Are you talking about Sabrina's old boyfriend? Your buddy, who's now an ob-gyn doc?"

It was Logan's turn to look startled. He recovered faster than Devon had, though. His smile widened into a rueful grin.

"I take it you're not Sabrina Russo."

"No, Mr. Logan, I am *not.*"

* * * * *

Be sure to look for
THE CEO'S CHRISTMAS PROPOSITION
by Merline Lovelace.
Available in November 2008
wherever books are sold,
including most bookstores, supermarkets,
drugstores and discount stores.

HARLEQUIN®

American ★ Romance®

LAURA MARIE ALTOM
A Daddy
for Christmas

THE STATE OF PARENTHOOD

Single mom Jesse Cummings is struggling
to run her Oklahoma ranch and raise her
two little girls after the death of her husband.
Then on Christmas Eve, a miracle strolls onto
her land in the form of tall, handsome bull
rider Gage Moore. He doesn't plan on staying,
but in the season of miracles, anything
can happen....

**Available November
wherever books are sold.**

LOVE, HOME & HAPPINESS

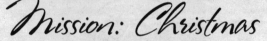

REQUEST YOUR FREE BOOKS!

2 FREE NOVELS PLUS 2 FREE GIFTS!

SPECIAL EDITION®

Life, Love and Family!

YES! Please send me 2 FREE Silhouette Special Edition® novels and my 2 FREE gifts (gifts are worth about $10). After receiving them, if I don't wish to receive any more books, I can return the shipping statement marked "cancel." If I don't cancel, I will receive 6 brand-new novels every month and be billed just $4.24 per book in the U.S. or $4.99 per book in Canada, plus 25¢ shipping and handling per book and applicable taxes, if any*. That's a savings of at least 15% off the cover price! I understand that accepting the 2 free books and gifts places me under no obligation to buy anything. I can always return a shipment and cancel at any time. Even if I never buy another book from Silhouette, the two free books and gifts are mine to keep forever.

235 SDN EEYU   335 SDN EEY6

Name	(PLEASE PRINT)	
Address		Apt. #
City	State/Prov.	Zip/Postal Code

Signature (if under 18, a parent or guardian must sign)

Mail to the **Silhouette Reader Service:**
IN U.S.A.: P.O. Box 1867, Buffalo, NY 14240-1867
IN CANADA: P.O. Box 609, Fort Erie, Ontario L2A 5X3

Not valid to current subscribers of Silhouette Special Edition books.

Want to try two free books from another line?
Call 1-800-873-8635 or visit www.morefreebooks.com.

* Terms and prices subject to change without notice. N.Y. residents add applicable sales tax. Canadian residents will be charged applicable provincial taxes and GST. Offer not valid in Quebec. This offer is limited to one order per household. All orders subject to approval. Credit or debit balances in a customer's account(s) may be offset by any other outstanding balance owed by or to the customer. Please allow 4 to 6 weeks for delivery. Offer available while quantities last.

Your Privacy: Silhouette is committed to protecting your privacy. Our Privacy Policy is available online at www.eHarlequin.com or upon request from the Reader Service. From time to time we make our lists of customers available to reputable third parties who may have a product or service of interest to you. If you would prefer we not share your name and address, please check here. ☐

SSE08R

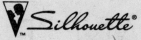
Silhouette®

COMING NEXT MONTH

SSECNM1008BPA